THE HAIRY ONES
SHALL DANCE

THE HAIRY ONES SHALL DANCE

GANS T. FIELD

WILDSIDE PRESS

INTRODUCTION

KARL WURF

Gans T. Field, an enigmatic figure in early 20th-century pulp fiction, is best remembered for his contributions to the legendary pulp magazine *Weird Tales*. Though details of his life remain scarce, Field's work has left an indelible mark on the horror genre. One of his notable stories, *The Hairy Ones Shall Dance*, delves into the chilling world of werewolves, a staple of supernatural fiction that has fascinated and terrified readers for centuries.

Weird Tales, first published in 1923, was a pioneering platform for horror and fantasy fiction. It introduced readers to a realm of macabre and fantastical stories, featuring writers like H.P. Lovecraft, Robert E. Howard, and Clark Ashton Smith. The magazine's unique blend of horror, fantasy, and the supernatural set it apart, making it a cornerstone of genre fiction. *The Hairy Ones Shall Dance* exemplifies the eerie and atmospheric storytelling that *Weird Tales* championed, drawing readers into a world where the ordinary meets the unthinkable.

* * * *

Werewolves, creatures that transform from human to wolf under the full moon, embody the primal fear of losing control to the beast within. This theme has been explored in countless tales, from folklore to modern horror, captivating audiences with its blend of mystery and terror. Classic literary examples include *The Werewolf* by Clemence Housman and *The Wolf Leader* by Alexandre Dumas.

Within the pages of *Weird Tales*, werewolf stories found a unique and eerie home. H. Warner Munn's *The Werewolf of Ponkert* is a notable example, weaving a tale of horror and transformation that thrilled readers. Another example is *Wolfshead* by Robert E. Howard, showcasing the magazine's penchant for macabre and thrilling narratives. These stories, among others, have cemented the werewolf's place in the pantheon of horror fiction, captivating readers with their dark allure.

FOREWORD

To Whom It May Concern:

Few words are best, as Sir Philip Sidney once wrote in challenging an enemy. The present account will be accepted as a challenge by the vast army of skeptics of which I once made one. Therefore I write it brief and bald. If my story seems unsteady in spots, that is because the hand that writes it still quivers from my recent ordeal.

Shifting the metaphor from duello to military engagement, this is but the first gun of the bombardment. Even now sworn statements are being prepared by all others who survived the strange and, in some degree, unthinkable adventure I am recounting. After that, every great psychic investigator in the country, as well as some from Europe, will begin researches. I wish that my friends and brother-magicians, Houdini and Thurston, had lived to bear a hand in them.

I must apologize for the strong admixture of the personal element in my narrative. Some may feel that I err against good taste. My humble argument is that I was not merely an observer, but an actor, albeit a clumsy one, throughout the drama.

As to the setting forth of matters which many will call impossible, let me smile in advance. Things happen and have always happened, that defy the narrow science of test-tube and formula. I can only say again that I am writing the truth, and that my statement will be supported by my companions in the adventure.

—Talbot Wills.

November 15, 1937.

CHAPTER 1

"WHY MUST THE BURDEN OF PROOF REST WITH THE SPIRITS?"

"You don't believe in psychic phenomena," said Doctor Otto Zoberg yet again, "because you *won't*."

This with studied kindness, sitting in the most comfortable chair of my hotel room. I, at thirty-four, silently hoped I would have his health and charm at fifty-four—he was so rugged for all his lean length, so well groomed for all his tweeds and beard and joined eyebrows, so articulate for all his accent. Doctor Zoberg quite apparently liked and admired me, and I felt guilty once more that I did not entirely return the compliment.

"I know that you are a stage magician—" he began afresh.

"I was once," I amended, a little sulkily. My early career had brought me considerable money and notice, but after the novelty of show business was worn off I had never rejoiced in it. Talboto the Mysterious—it had been impressive, but tawdry. Better to be Talbot Wills, lecturer and investigator in the field of exposing fraudulent mediums.

For six years I had known Doctor Otto Zoberg, the champion of spiritism and mediumism, as rival and companion. We had first met in debate under auspices of the Society for Psychical Research in London. I, young enough for enthusiasm but also for carelessness, had been badly out-thought and out-talked. But afterward, Doctor Zoberg had praised my arguments and my delivery, and had graciously taken me out to a late supper. The following day, there arrived from him a present of helpful books and magazines. Our next platform duel found me in a position to get a little of my own back; and he, afterward, laughingly congratulated me on turning to account the material he had sent me. After that, we were public foemen and personal inseparables. Just now we were touring the United States, debating, giving exhibitions, visiting mediums. The night's program, before a Washington audience liberally laced with high officials, had ended in what we agreed was a draw; and here we were, squabbling good-naturedly afterward.

"Please, Doctor," I begged, offering him a cigarette, "save your charges of stubbornness for the theater."

He waved my case aside and bit the end from a villainous black cheroot. "I wouldn't say it, here or in public, if it weren't true, Talbot. Yet you sneer even at telepathy, and only half believe in mental suggestion. *Ach*, you are worse than Houdini."

"Houdini was absolutely sincere," I almost blazed, for I had known and worshipped that brilliant and kindly prince of conjurers and fraud-finders.

"*Ach*, to be sure, to be sure," nodded Zoberg over his blazing match. "I did not say he was not. Yet, he refused proof—the proof that he himself embodied. Houdini was a great mystic, a medium. His power for miracles he did not know himself."

I had heard that before, from Conan Doyle as well as Zoberg, but I made no comment. Zoberg continued:

"Perhaps Houdini was afraid—if anything could frighten so brave and wise a man it would assuredly come from within. And so he would not even listen to argument." He turned suddenly somber. "Perhaps he knew best, *ja*. But he was stubborn, and so are you."

"I don't think you can say that of me," I objected once more. The cheroot was alight now, and I kindled a cigarette to combat in some degree the gunpowdery fumes.

Teeth gleamed amiably through the beard, and Zoberg nodded again, in frank delight this time. "Oh, we have hopes of you, Wills, where we gave up Houdini."

He had never said that before, not so plainly at any rate. I smiled back. "I've always been willing to be shown. Give me a fool-proof, fake-proof, supernormal phenomenon, Doctor; let me convince myself; then I'll come gladly into the spiritist camp."

"*Ach*, so you always say!" he exploded, but without genuine wrath. "Why must the burden of proof rest with the spirits? How can you prove that they do not live and move and act? Study what Eddington has to say about that."

"For five years," I reminded him, "I have offered a prize of five thousand dollars to any medium whose spirit miracles I could not duplicate by honest sleight-of-hand."

He gestured with slim fingers, as though to push the words back into me. "That proves absolutely nothing, Wills. For all your skill, do you think that sleight-of-hand can be the only way? Is it even the best way?"

"I've unmasked famous mediums for years, at the rate of one a month," I flung back. "Unmasked them as the clumsiest of fakes."

"Because some are dishonest, are all dishonest?" he appealed. "What specific thing would convince you, my friend?"

I thought for a moment, gazing at him through the billows of smoke. Not a gray hair to him—and I, twenty years his junior, had six or eight at either temple. I went on to admire and even to envy that pointed trowel of beard, the sort of thing that I, a magician, might have cultivated once. Then I made my answer.

"I'd ask for a materialization, Doctor. An ectoplasmic apparition, visible and solid to touch—in an empty room with no curtains or closets, all entrances sealed by myself, the medium and witnesses shackled." He started to open his mouth, but I hurried to prevent him. "I know what you'll say—that I've seen a number of impressive ectoplasms. So I have, perhaps, but not one was scientifically and dispassionately controlled. No, Doctor, if I'm to be convinced, I must make the conditions and set the stage myself."

"And if the materialization was a complete success?"

"Then it would prove the claim to me—to the world. Materializations are the most important question in the whole field."

He looked long at me, narrowing his shrewd eyes beneath the dark single bar of his brows. "Wills," he said at length, "I hoped you would ask something like this."

"You did?"

"*Ja.* Because—first, can you spare a day or so?"

I replied guardedly, "I can, I believe. We have two weeks or more before the New Orleans date." I computed rapidly. "Yes, that's December 8. What have you got up your sleeve, Doctor?"

He grinned once more, with a great display of gleaming white teeth, and flung out his long arms. "My sleeves, you will observe, are empty!" he cried. "No trickery. But within five hours of where we sit—five hours by fast automobile—is a little town. And in that town there is a little medium. No, Wills, you have never seen or heard of her. It is only myself who found her by chance, who studied her long and prayerfully. Come with me, Wills—she will teach you how little you know and how much you can learn!"

CHAPTER 2

"YOU CAN ALMOST HEAR THE GHOSTS."

I have sat down with the purpose of writing out, plainly and even flatly, all that happened to me and to Doctor Otto Zoberg in our impromptu adventure at psychic investigation; yet, almost at the start, I find it necessary to be vague about the tiny town where that adventure ran its course. Zoberg began by refusing to tell me its name, and now my friends of various psychical research committees have asked me to hold my peace until they have finished certain examinations without benefit of yellow journals or prying politicians.

It is located, as Zoberg told me, within five hours by fast automobile of Washington. On the following morning, after a quick and early breakfast, we departed at seven o'clock in my sturdy coupé. I drove and Zoberg guided. In the turtle-back we had stowed bags, for the November sky had begun to boil up with dark, heavy clouds, and a storm might delay us.

On the way Zoberg talked a great deal, with his usual charm and animation. He scoffed at my skepticism and prophesied my conversion before another midnight.

"A hundred years ago, realists like yourself were ridiculing hypnotism," he chuckled. "They thought that it was a fantastic fake, like one of Edgar Poe's amusing tales, *ja*? And now it is a great science, for healing and comforting the world. A few years ago, the world scorned mental telepathy—"

"Hold on," I interrupted. "I'm none too convinced of it now."

"I said just that, last night. However, you think that there is some grain of truth to it. You would be a fool to laugh at the many experiments in clairvoyance carried on at Duke University."

"Yes, they are impressive," I admitted.

"They are tremendous, and by no means unique," he insisted. "Think of a number between one and ten," he said suddenly.

I gazed at my hands on the wheel, thought of a joking reply, then fell in with his mood.

"All right," I replied. "I'm thinking of a number. What is it?"

"It is seven," he cried out at once, then laughed heartily at the blank look on my face.

"Look here, that's a logical number for an average man to think of," I protested. "You relied on human nature, not telepathy."

He grinned and tweaked the end of his beard between manicured fingers. "Very good, Wills, try again. A color this time."

I paused a moment before replying, "All right, guess what it is."

He, too, hesitated, staring at me sidewise. "I think it is blue," he offered at length.

"Go to the head of the class," I grumbled. "I rather expected you to guess red—that's most obvious."

"But I was not guessing," he assured me. "A flash of blue came before my mind's eye. Come, let us try another time."

We continued the experiment for a while. Zoberg was not always correct, but he was surprizingly close in nearly every case. The most interesting results were with the names of persons, and Zoberg achieved some rather mystifying approximations. Thus, when I was thinking of the actor Boris Karloff, he gave me the name of the actor Bela Lugosi. Upon my thinking of Gilbert K. Chesterton, he named Chesterton's close friend Hilaire Belloc, and my concentration on George Bernard Shaw brought forth a shout of "Santa Claus." When I reiterated my charge of psychological trickery and besought him to teach me his method, he grew actually angry and did not speak for more than half an hour. Then he began to discuss our destination.

"A most amazing community," he pronounced. "It is old—one of the oldest inland towns of all America. Wait until you see the houses, my friend. You can almost hear the ghosts within them, in broad daylight. And their Devil's Croft, that is worth seeing, too."

"Their what?"

He shook his head, as though in despair. "And you set yourself up as an authority on occultism!" he sniffed. "Next you will admit that you have never heard of the Druids. A Devil's Croft, my dull young friend, used to be part of every English or Scots village. The good people would set aside a field for Satan, so that he would not take their own lands."

"And this settlement has such a place?"

"*Ja wohl*, a grove of the thickest timber ever seen in this over-civilized country, and hedged in to boot. I do not say that they believe, but it is civic property and protected by special order from trespassers."

"I'd like to visit that grove," I said.

"I pray you!" he cried, waving in protest. "Do not make us unwelcome."

* * * *

We arrived shortly before noon. The little town rests in a circular hollow among high wooded hills, and there is not a really good road into it, for two or three miles around. After listening to Zoberg, I had expected something grotesque or forbidding, but I was disappointed. The houses were sturdy and modest, in some cases poor. The greater part of them made a close-huddled mass, like a herd of cattle threatened by wolves, with here and there an isolated dwelling like an adventuresome young fighting-bull. The streets were narrow, crooked and unpaved, and for once in this age I saw buggies and wagons outnumbering automobiles. The central square, with a two-story town hall of red brick and a hideous cast-iron war memorial, still boasted numerous hitching-rails, brown with age and smooth with use. There were few real signs of modern progress. For instance, the drug store was a shabby clapboard affair with "Pharmacy" painted upon its windows, and it sold only drugs, soda and tobacco; while the one hotel was low and rambling and bore the title "Luther Inn." I heard that the population was three hundred and fifty, but I am inclined to think it was closer to three hundred.

We drew up in front of the Luther Inn, and a group of roughly dressed men gazed at us with the somewhat hostile interrogation that often marks a rural American community at the approach of strangers. These men wore mail-order coats of corduroy or suede—the air was growing nippier by the minute— and plow shoes or high laced boots under dungaree pants. All of them were of Celtic or Anglo-Saxon type.

"Hello!" cried Zoberg jovially. "I see you there, my friend Mr. Gird. How is your charming daughter?"

The man addressed took a step forward from the group on the porch. He was a raw-boned, grizzled native with pale, pouched eyes, and was a trifle better dressed than the others, in a rather ministerial coat of dark cloth and a wide black hat. He cleared his throat before replying.

"Hello, Doctor. Susan's well, thanks. What do you want of us?"

It was a definite challenge, that would repel or anger most men, but Zoberg was not to be denied. He scrambled out of the car and cordially shook the hand of the man he had called Mr. Gird. Meanwhile he spoke in friendly fashion to one or two of the others.

"And here," he wound up, "is a very good friend of mine, Mr. Talbot Wills."

All eyes—and very unfriendly eyes they were, as a whole— turned upon me. I got out slowly, and at Zoberg's insistence shook hands with Gird. Finally the grizzled man came with us to the car.

"I promised you once," he said glumly to Zoberg, "that I would let you and Susan dig as deeply as you wanted to into this matter of spirits. I've often wished since that I hadn't, but my word was never broken yet. Come along with me; Susan is cooking dinner, and there'll be enough for all of us."

He got into the car with us, and as we drove out of the square and toward his house he conversed quietly with Zoberg and me.

"Yes," he answered one of my questions, "the houses are old, as you can see. Some of them have stood since the Revolutionary War with England, and our town's ordinances have stood longer than that. You aren't the first to be impressed, Mr. Wills. Ten years ago a certain millionaire came and said he wanted to endow us, so that we would stay as we are. He had a lot to say about native color and historical value. We told him that we would stay as we are without having to take money from him, or from anybody else for that matter."

* * * *

Gird's home was large but low, all one story, and of darkly painted clapboards over heavy timbers. The front door was hung on the most massive hand-wrought hinges. Gird knocked at it, and a slender, smallish girl opened to us.

She wore a woolen dress, as dark as her father's coat, with white at the neck and wrists. Her face, under masses of thunder-black hair, looked Oriental at first glance, what with high cheek-bones and eyes set aslant; then I saw that her eyes were a bright gray like worn silver, and her skin rosy, with a firm chin and a generous mouth. The features were representatively Celtic, after all, and I wondered for perhaps the fiftieth time in my life if there was some sort of blood link between Scot and Mongol. Her hand, on the brass knob of the door, showed as slender and white as some evening flower.

"Susan," said Gird, "here's Doctor Zoberg. And this is his friend, Mr. Wills."

She smiled at Zoberg, then nodded to me, respectfully and rather shyly.

"My daughter," Gird finished the introduction. "Well, dinner must be ready."

She led us inside. The parlor was rather plainer than in most old-fashioned provincial houses, but it was comfortable enough. Much of its furniture would have delighted antique dealers, and one or two pieces would have impressed museum directors. The dining-room beyond had plate-racks on the walls and a long table of dark wood, with high-backed chairs. We had some fried ham, biscuits, coffee and stewed fruit that must have been home-canned. Doctor Zoberg and Gird ate heartily, talking of local trifles, but Susan Gird hardly touched her food. I, watching her with stealthy admiration, forgot to take more than a few mouthfuls.

After the repast she carried out the dishes and we men returned to the parlor. Gird faced us.

"You're here for some more hocus-pocus?" he hazarded gruffly.

"For another séance," amended Zoberg, suave as ever.

"Doctor," said Gird, "I think this had better be the last time."

Zoberg held out a hand in pleading protest, but Gird thrust his own hands behind him and looked sternly stubborn. "It's not good for the girl," he announced definitely.

"But she is a great medium—greater than Eusapia Paladino, or Daniel Home," Zoberg argued earnestly. "She is an important figure in the psychic world, lost and wasted here in this backwater—"

"Please don't miscall our town," interrupted Gird. "Well, Doctor, I agree to a final séance, as you call it. But I'm going to be present."

Zoberg made a gesture as of refusal, but I sided with Gird.

"If this is to be my test, I want another witness," I told Zoberg.

"*Ach!* If it is a success, you will say that he helped to deceive."

"Not I. I'll arrange things so there will be no deception."

Both Zoberg and Gird stared at me. I wondered which of them was the more disdainful of my confidence.

Then Susan Gird joined us, and for once I wanted to speak of other subjects than the occult.

CHAPTER 3

"THAT THING ISN'T MY DAUGHTER—"

It was Zoberg who suggested that I take Susan Gird for a relaxing drive in my car. I acclaimed the idea as a brilliant one, and she, thanking me quietly, put on an archaic-seeming cloak, black and heavy. We left her father and Zoberg talking idly and drove slowly through the town.

She pointed out to me the Devil's Croft of which I had heard from the doctor, and I saw it to be a grove of trees, closely and almost rankly set. It stood apart from the sparser timber on the hills, and around it stretched bare fields. Their emptiness suggested that all the capacity for life had been drained away and poured into that central clump. No road led near to it, and I was obliged to content myself by idling the car at a distance while we gazed and she talked.

"It's evergreen, of course," I said. "Cedar and a little juniper."

"Only in the hedge around it," Susan Gird informed me. "It was planted by the town council about ten years ago."

I stared. "But surely there's greenness in the center, too," I argued.

"Perhaps. They say that the leaves never fall, even in January."

I gazed at what appeared to be a little fluff of white mist above it, the whiter by contrast with the black clouds that lowered around the hill-tops. To my questions about the town council, Susan Gird told me some rather curious things about the government of the community. There were five councilmen, elected every year, and no mayor. Each of the five presided at a meeting in turn. Among the ordinances enforced by the council was one providing for support of the single church.

"I should think that such an ordinance could be set aside as illegal," I observed.

"I think it could," she agreed, "but nobody has ever wished to try."

The minister of the church, she continued, was invariably a member of the council. No such provision appeared on the town records, nor was it even urged as a "written law," but it had always been deferred to. The single peace officer of the town, she continued, was the duly elected constable. He was always commissioned as deputy sheriff by officials at the county seat, and his duties included census taking, tax collecting and similar matters. The only other officer with a state commission was the justice; and her father, John Gird, had held that post for the last six years.

"He's an attorney, then?" I suggested, but Susan Gird shook her head.

"The only attorney in this place is a retired judge, Keith Pursuivant," she informed me. "He came from some other part of the world, and he appears in town about once a month—lives out yonder past the Croft. As a matter of fact, an ordinary experience of law isn't enough for our peculiar little government."

She spoke of her fellow-townsmen as quiet, simple folk who were content for the most part to keep to themselves, and then, yielding to my earnest pleas, she told me something of herself.

The Gird family counted its descent from an original settler—though she was not exactly sure of when or how the settlement was made—and had borne a leading part in community affairs through more than two centuries. Her mother, who had died when Susan Gird was seven, had been a stranger; an "outlander" was the local term for such, and I think it is used in Devonshire, which may throw light on the original founders of the community. Apparently this woman had shown some tendencies toward psychic power, for she had several times prophesied coming events or told neighbors where to find lost things. She was well loved for her labors in caring for the sick, and indeed she had died from a fever contracted when tending the victims of an epidemic.

"Doctor Zoberg had known her," Susan Gird related. "He came here several years after her death, and seemed badly shaken when he heard what had happened. He and Father became good friends, and he has been kind to me, too. I remember his saying, the first time we met, that I looked like Mother and that it was apparent that I had inherited her spirit."

She had grown up and spent three years at a teachers' college, but left before graduation, refusing a position at a school so that she could keep house for her lonely father. Still idiotically mannerless, I mentioned the possibility of her marrying some young man of the town. She laughed musically.

"Why, I stopped thinking of marriage when I was fourteen!" she cried. Then, "Look, it's snowing."

So it was, and I thought it time to start for her home. We finished the drive on the best of terms, and when we reached her home in midafternoon, we were using first names.

* * * *

Gird, I found, had capitulated to Doctor Zoberg's genial insistence. From disliking the thought of a séance, he had come to savor the prospect of witnessing it—Zoberg had always excluded him before. Gird had even picked up a metaphysical term or two from listening to the doctor, and with these he spiced his normally plain speech.

"This ectoplasm stuff sounds reasonable," he admitted. "If there is any such thing, there could be ghosts, couldn't there?"

Zoberg twinkled, and tilted his beard-spike forward. "You will find that Mr. Wills does not believe in ectoplasm."

"Nor do I believe that the production of ectoplasm would prove existence of a ghost," I added. "What do you say, Miss Susan?"

She smiled and shook her dark head. "To tell you the truth, I'm aware only dimly of what goes on during a séance."

"Most mediums say that," nodded Zoberg sagely.

As the sun set and the darkness came down, we prepared for the experiment.

The dining-room was chosen, as the barest and quietest room in the house. First I made a thorough examination, poking into corners, tapping walls and handling furniture, to the accompaniment of jovial taunts from Zoberg. Then, to his further amusement, I produced from my grip a big lump of sealing-wax, and with this I sealed both the kitchen and parlor doors, stamping the wax with my signet ring. I also closed, latched and sealed the windows, on the sills of which little heaps of snow had begun to collect.

"You're kind of making sure, Mr. Wills," said Gird, lighting a patent carbide lamp.

"That's because I take this business seriously," I replied, and Zoberg clapped his hands in approval.

"Now," I went on, "off with your coats and vests, gentlemen."

Gird and Zoberg complied, and stood up in their shirt-sleeves. I searched and felt them both all over. Gird was a trifle bleak in manner, Zoberg gay and bright-faced. Neither had any concealed apparatus, I made sure. My next move was to set a chair against the parlor door, seal its legs to the floor, and instruct Gird to sit in it. He did so, and I produced a pair of handcuffs from my bag and shackled his left wrist to the arm of the chair.

"Capital!" cried Zoberg. "Do not be so sour, Mr. Gird. I would not trust handcuffs on Mr. Wills—he was once a magician and knows all the escape tricks."

"Your turn's coming, Doctor," I assured him.

Against the opposite wall and facing Gird's chair I set three more chairs, melting wax around their legs and stamping it. Then I dragged all other furniture far away, arranging it against the kitchen door. Finally I asked Susan to take the central chair of the three, seated Zoberg at her left hand and myself at her right. Beside me, on the floor, I set the carbide lamp.

"With your permission," I said, and produced more manacles. First I fastened Susan's left ankle to Zoberg's right, then her left wrist to his right. Zoberg's left wrist I chained to his chair, leaving him entirely helpless.

"What thick wrists you have!" I commented. "I never knew they were so sinewy."

"You never chained them before," he grinned.

With two more pairs of handcuffs I shackled my own left wrist and ankle to Susan on the right.

"Now we are ready," I pronounced.

"You've treated us like bank robbers," muttered Gird.

"No, no, do not blame Mr. Wills," Zoberg defended me again. He looked anxiously at Susan. "Are you quite prepared, my dear?"

Her eyes met his for a long moment; then she closed them and nodded. I, bound to her, felt a relaxation of her entire body. After a moment she bowed her chin upon her breast.

"Let nobody talk," warned Zoberg softly. "I think that this will be a successful venture. Wills, the light."

With my free hand I turned it out.

All was intensely dark for a moment. Then, as my eyes adjusted themselves, the room seemed to lighten. I could see the deep gray rectangles of the windows, the snow at their bottoms, the blurred outline of the man in his chair across the floor from me, the form of Susan at my left hand. My ears, likewise sharpening, detected the girl's gentle breathing, as if she slept. Once or twice her right hand twitched, shaking my own arm in its manacle. It was as though she sought to attract my attention.

Before and a little beyond her, something pale and cloudy was making itself visible. Even as I fixed my gaze upon it, I heard something that sounded like a gusty panting. It might have been a tired dog or other beast. The pallid mist was changing shape and substance, too, and growing darker. It shifted against the dim light from the windows, and I had a momentary impression of something erect but misshapen—misshapen in an animal way. Was that a head? And were those pointed ears, or part of a head-dress? I told myself determinedly that this was a clever illusion, successful despite my precautions.

"Something pale and cloudy was making itself visible."

It moved, and I heard a rattle upon the planks. Claws, or perhaps hobnails. Did not Gird wear heavy boots? Yet he was surely sitting in his chair; I saw something shift position at that point. The grotesque form had come before me, crouching or creeping.

Despite my self-assurance that this was a trick, I could not govern the chill that swept over me. The thing had come to a halt close to me, was lifting itself as a hound that paws its master's knees. I was aware of an odor, strange and disagreeable, like the wind from a great beast's cage. Then the paws were upon my lap—indeed, they were not paws. I felt them grip my legs, with fingers and opposable thumbs. A sniffing muzzle thrust almost into my face, and upon its black snout a dim, wet gleam was manifest.

Then Gird, from his seat across the room, screamed hoarsely.

"That thing isn't my daughter—"

In the time it took him to rip out those five words, the huddled monster at my knees whirled back and away from me, reared for a trice like a deformed giant, and leaped across the intervening space upon him. I saw that Gird had tried to rise, his chained wrist hampering him. Then his voice broke in the midst of what he was trying to say; he made a choking sound and the thing emitted a barking growl.

Tearing loose from its wax fastenings, the chair fell upon its side. There was a struggle and a clatter, and Gird squealed like a rabbit in a trap. The attacker fell away from him toward us.

It was all over before one might ask what it was about.

CHAPTER 4

"I DON'T KNOW WHAT KILLED HIM."

Just when I got up I do not remember, but I was on my feet as the grapplers separated. Without thinking of danger—and surely danger was there in the room—I might have rushed forward; but Susan Gird, lying limp in her chair, hampered me in our mutual shackles. Standing where I was, then, I pawed in my pocket for something I had not mentioned to her or to Zoberg; an electric torch.

It fitted itself into my hand, a compact little cylinder, and I whipped it out with my finger on the switch. A cone of white light spurted across the room, making a pool about and upon the motionless form of Gird. He lay crumpled on one side, his back toward us, and a smudge of black wetness was widening about his slack head and shoulders.

With the beam I swiftly quartered the room, probing it into every corner and shadowed nook. The creature that had attacked Gird had utterly vanished. Susan Gird now gave a soft moan, like a dreamer of dreadful things. I flashed my light her way.

It flooded her face and she quivered under the impact of the glare, but did not open her eyes. Beyond her I saw Zoberg, doubled forward in his bonds. He was staring blackly at the form of Gird, his eyes protruding and his clenched teeth showing through his beard.

"Doctor Zoberg!" I shouted at him, and his face jerked nervously toward me. It was fairly cross-hatched with tense lines, and as white as fresh pipe-clay. He tried to say something, but his voice would not command itself.

Dropping the torch upon the floor, I next dug keys from my pocket and with trembling haste unlocked the irons from Susan Gird's wrist and ankle on my side. Then, stepping hurriedly to Zoberg, I made him sit up and freed him as speedily as possible. Finally I returned, found my torch again and stepped across to Gird.

My first glance at close quarters was enough; he was stone-dead, with his throat torn brutally out. His cheeks, too, were ripped in parallel gashes, as though by the grasp of claws or nails. Radiance suddenly glowed behind me, and Zoberg moved forward, holding up the carbide lamp.

"I found this beside your chair," he told me unsteadily. "I found a match and lighted it." He looked down at Gird, and his lips twitched, as though he would be hysterical.

"Steady, Doctor," I cautioned him sharply, and took the lamp from him. "See what you can do for Gird."

He stooped slowly, as though he had grown old. I stepped to one side, putting the lamp on the table. Zoberg spoke again:

"It is absolutely no use, Wills. We can do nothing. Gird has been killed."

I had turned my attention to the girl. She still sagged in her chair, breathing deeply and rhythmically as if in untroubled slumber.

"Susan," I called her. "Susan!"

She did not stir, and Doctor Zoberg came back to where I bent above her. "Susan," he whispered penetratingly, "wake up, child."

Her eyes unveiled themselves slowly, and looked up at us. "What—" she began drowsily.

"Prepare yourself," I cautioned her quickly. "Something has happened to your father."

She stared across at Gird's body, and then she screamed, tremulously and long. Zoberg caught her in his arms, and she swayed and shuddered against their supporting circle. From her own wrists my irons still dangled, and they clanked as she wrung her hands in aimless distraction.

Going to the dead man once more, I unchained him from the chair and turned him upon his back. Susan's black cloak lay upon one of the other chairs, and I picked it up and spread it above him. Then I went to each door in turn, and to the windows.

"The seals are unbroken," I reported. "There isn't a space through which even a mouse could slip in or out. Yet—"

"I did it!" wailed Susan suddenly. "Oh, my God, what dreadful thing came out of me to murder my father!"

* * * *

I unfastened the parlor door and opened it. Almost at the same time a loud knock sounded from the front of the house.

Zoberg lifted his head, nodding to me across Susan's trembling shoulder. His arms were still clasped around her, and I could not help but notice that they seemed thin and ineffectual now. When I had chained them, I had wondered at their steely cording. Had this awful calamity drained him of strength?

"Go," he said hoarsely. "See who it is."

I went. Opening the front door, I came face to face with a tall, angular silhouette in a slouch hat with snow on the brim.

"Who are you?" I jerked out, startled.

"O'Bryant," boomed back an organ-deep bass. "What's the fuss here?"

"Well—" I began, then hesitated.

"Stranger in town, ain't you?" was the next question. "I saw you when you stopped at the Luther Inn. I'm O'Bryant—the constable."

He strode across the door-sill, peered about him in the dark, and then slouched into the lighted dining-room. Following, I made him out as a stern, roughly dressed man of forty or so, with a lean face made strong by a salient chin and a simitar nose. His light blue eyes studied the still form of John Gird, and he stooped to draw away the cloak. Susan gave another agonized cry, and I heard Zoberg gasp as if deeply shocked. The constable, too, flinched and replaced the cloak more quickly than he had taken it up.

"Who done that?" he barked at me.

Again I found it hard to answer. Constable O'Bryant sniffed suspiciously at each of us in turn, took up the lamp and herded us into the parlor. There he made us take seats.

"I want to know everything about this business," he said harshly. "You," he flung at me, "you seem to be the closest to sensible. Give me the story, and don't leave out a single bit of it."

Thus commanded, I made shift to describe the séance and what had led up to it. I was as uneasy as most innocent people are when unexpectedly questioned by peace officers. O'Bryant interrupted twice with a guttural "Huh!" and once with a credulous whistle.

"And this killing happened in the dark?" he asked when I had finished. "Well, which of you dressed up like a devil and done it?"

Susan whimpered and bowed her head. Zoberg, outraged, sprang to his feet.

"It was a creature from another world," he protested angrily. "None of us had a reason to kill Mr. Gird."

O'Bryant emitted a sharp, equine laugh. "Don't go to tell me any ghost stories, Doctor Zoberg. We folks have heard a lot about the hocus-pocus you've pulled off here from time to time. Looks like it might have been to cover up some kind of rough stuff."

"How could it be?" demanded Zoberg. "Look here, Constable, these handcuffs." He held out one pair of them. "We were all confined with them, fastened to chairs that were sealed to the floor. Mr. Gird was also chained, and his chair made fast out of our reach. Go into the next room and look for yourself."

"Let me see them irons," grunted O'Bryant, snatching them.

He turned them over and over in his hands, snapped them shut, tugged and pressed, then held out a hand for my keys. Unlocking the cuffs, he peered into the clamping mechanism.

"These are regulation bracelets," he pronounced. "You were all chained up, then?"

"We were," replied Zoberg, and both Susan and I nodded.

Into the constable's blue eyes came a sudden shrewd light. "I guess you must have been, at that. But did you stay that way?" He whipped suddenly around, bending above my chair to fix his gaze upon me. "How about you, Mr. Wills?"

"Of course we stayed that way," I replied.

"Yeh? Look here, ain't you a professional magician?"

"How did you know that?" I asked.

He grinned widely and without warmth. "The whole town's been talking about you, Mr. Wills. A stranger can't be here all day without his whole record coming out." The grin vanished. "You're a magician, all right, and you can get out of handcuffs. Ain't that so?"

"Of course it's so," Zoberg answered for me. "But why should that mean that my friend has killed Mr. Gird?"

O'Bryant wagged his head in triumph. "That's what we'll find out later. Right now it adds up very simple. Gird was killed, in a room that was all sealed up. Three other folks was in with him, all handcuffed to their chairs. Which of them got loose without the others catching on?" He nodded brightly at me, as if in answer to his own question.

Zoberg gave me a brief, penetrating glance, then seemed to shrivel up in his own chair. He looked almost as exhausted as Susan. I, too, was feeling near to collapse.

"You want to own up, Mr. Wills?" invited O'Bryant.

"I certainly do not," I snapped at him. "You've got the wrong man."

"I thought," he made answer, as though catching me in a damaging admission, "that it was a devil, not a man, who killed Gird."

I shook my head. "I don't know what killed him."

"Maybe you'll remember after a while." He turned toward the door, "You come along with me. I'm going to lock you up."

I rose with a sigh of resignation, but paused for a moment to address Zoberg. "Get hold of yourself," I urged him. "Get somebody in here to look after Miss Susan, and then clarify in your mind what happened. You can help me prove that it wasn't I."

Zoberg nodded very wearily, but did not look up.

"Don't neither of you go into that room where the body is," O'Bryant warned them. "Mr. Wills, get your coat and hat."

I did so, and we left the house. The snow was inches deep and still falling. O'Bryant led me across the street and knocked on the door of a peak-roofed house. A swarthy little man opened to us.

"There's been a murder, Jim," said O'Bryant importantly. "Over at Gird's. You're deputized—go and keep watch. Better take the missus along, to look after Susan. She's bad cut up about it."

We left the new deputy in charge and walked down the street, then turned into the square. Two or three men standing in front of the "Pharmacy" stared curiously, then whispered as we passed. Another figure paused to give me a searching glance. I was not too stunned to be irritated.

"Who are those?" I asked the constable.

"Town fellows," he informed me. "They're mighty interested to see what a killer looks like."

"How do they know about the case?" I almost groaned.

He achieved his short, hard laugh.

"Didn't I say that news travels fast in a town like this? Half the folks are talking about the killing this minute."

"You'll find you made a mistake," I assured him.

"If I have, I'll beg your pardon handsome. Meanwhile, I'll do my duty."

We were at the red brick town hall by now. At O'Bryant's side I mounted the granite steps and waited while he unlocked the big double door with a key the size of a can-opener.

"We're a kind of small town," he observed, half apologetically, "but there's a cell upstairs for you. Take off your hat and overcoat—you're staying inside till further notice."

CHAPTER 5

"THEY WANT TO TAKE THE LAW
INTO THEIR OWN HANDS."

The cell was an upper room of the town hall, with a heavy wooden door and a single tiny window. The walls were of bare, unplastered brick, the floor of concrete and the ceiling of white-washed planks. An oil lamp burned in a bracket. The only furniture was an iron bunk hinged to the wall just below the window, a wire-bound straight chair and an unpainted table. On top of this last stood a bowl and pitcher, with playing-cards scattered around them.

Constable O'Bryant locked me in and peered through a small grating in the door. He was all nose and eyes and wide lips, like a sardonic Punchinello.

"Look here," I addressed him suddenly, for the first time controlling my frayed nerves; "I want a lawyer."

"There ain't no lawyer in town," he boomed sourly.

"Isn't there a Judge Pursuivant in the neighborhood?" I asked, remembering something that Susan had told me.

"He don't practise law," O'Bryant grumbled, and his beaked face slid out of sight.

I turned to the table, idly gathered up the cards into a pack and shuffled them. To steady my still shaky fingers, I produced a few simple sleight-of-hand effects, palming of aces, making a king rise to the top, and springing the pack accordion-wise from one hand to the other.

"I'd sure hate to play poker with you," volunteered O'Bryant, who had come again to gaze at me.

I crossed to the grating and looked through at him. "You've got the wrong man," I said once more. "Even if I were guilty, you couldn't keep me from talking to a lawyer."

"Well, I'm doing it, ain't I?" he taunted me. "You wait until tomorrow and we'll go to the county seat. The sheriff can do whatever he wants to about a lawyer for you."

He ceased talking and listened. I heard the sound, too—a hoarse, dull murmur as of coal in a chute, or a distant, lowing herd of troubled cattle.

"What's that?" I asked him.

O'Bryant, better able to hear in the corridor, cocked his lean head for a moment. Then he cleared his throat. "Sounds like a lot of people talking, out in the square," he replied. "I wonder—"

He broke off quickly and walked away. The murmur was growing. I, pressing close to the grating to follow the constable with my eyes, saw that his shoulders were squared and his hanging fists doubled, as though he were suddenly aware of a lurking danger.

He reached the head of the stairs and clumped down, out of my sight. I turned back to the cell, walked to the bunk and, stepping upon it, raised the window. To the outside of the wooden frame two flat straps of iron had been securely bolted to act as bars. To these I clung as I peered out.

I was looking from the rear of the hall toward the center of the square, with the war memorial and the far line of shops and houses seen dimly through a thick curtain of falling snow. Something dark moved closer to the wall beneath, and I heard a cry, as if of menace.

"I see his head in the window!" bawled a voice, and more cries greeted this statement. A moment later a heavy missile hit the wall close to the frame.

I dropped back from the window and went once more to the grating of the door. Through it I saw O'Bryant coming back, accompanied by several men. They came close and peered through at me.

"Let me out," I urged. "That's a mob out there."

O'Bryant nodded dolefully. "Nothing like this ever happened here before," he said, as if he were responsible for the town's whole history of violence. "They act like they want to take the law into their own hands."

A short, fat man spoke at his elbow. "We're members of the town council, Mr. Wills. We heard that some of the citizens were getting ugly. We came here to look after you. We promise full protection."

"Amen," intoned a thinner specimen, whom I guessed to be the preacher.

"There are only half a dozen of you," I pointed out. "Is that enough to guard me from a violent mob?"

As if to lend significance to my question, from below and in front of the building came a great shout, compounded of many voices. Then a loud pounding echoed through the corridor, like a bludgeon on stout panels.

"You locked the door, Constable?" asked the short man.

"Sure I did," nodded O'Bryant.

A perfect rain of buffets sounded from below, then a heavy impact upon the front door of the hall. I could hear the hinges creak.

"They're trying to break the door down," whispered one of the council.

The short man turned resolutely on his heel. "There's a window at the landing of the stairs," he said. "Let's go and try to talk to them from that."

The whole party followed him away, and I could hear their feet on the stairs, then the lifting of a heavy window-sash. A loud and prolonged yelling came to my ears, as if the gathering outside had sighted and recognized a line of heads on the sill above them.

"Fellow citizens!" called the stout man's voice, but before he could go on a chorus of cries and hoots drowned him out. I could hear more thumps and surging shoves at the creaking door.

Escape I must. I whipped around and fairly ran to the bunk, mounting it a second time for a peep from my window. Nobody was visible below; apparently those I had seen previously had run to the front of the hall, there to hear the bellowings of the officials and take a hand in forcing the door.

Once again I dropped to the floor and began to tug at the fastenings of the bunk. It was an open oblong of metal, a stout frame of rods strung with springy wire netting. It could be folded upward against the wall and held with a catch, or dropped down with two lengths of chain to keep it horizontal. I dragged the mattress and blankets from it, then began a close examination of the chains. They were stoutly made, but the screw-plates that held them to the brick wall might be loosened. Clutching one chain with both my hands, I tugged with all my might, a foot braced against the wall. A straining heave, and it came loose.

At the same moment an explosion echoed through the corridor at my back, and more shouts rang through the air. Either O'Bryant or the mob had begun to shoot. Then a rending crash shook the building, and I heard one of the councilmen shouting: "Another like that and the door will be down!"

His words inspired additional speed within me. I took the loose end of the chain in my hand. Its links were of twisted iron, and the final one had been sawed through to admit the loop of the screw-plate, then clamped tight again. But my frantic tugging had widened this narrow cut once more, and quickly I freed it from the dangling plate. Then, folding the bunk against the wall, I drew the chain upward. It would just reach to the window—that open link would hook around one of the flat bars.

* * * *

The noise of breakage rang louder in the front of the building. Once more I heard the voice of the short councilman: "I command you all to go home, before Constable O'Bryant fires on you again!"

"We got guns, too!" came back a defiant shriek, and in proof of this statement came a rattle of shots. I heard an agonized moan, and the voice of the minister: "Are you hit?"

"In the shoulder," was O'Bryant's deep, savage reply.

My chain fast to the bar, I pulled back and down on the edge of the bunk. It gave some leverage, but not enough—the bar was fastened too solidly. Desperate, I clambered upon the iron framework. Gaining the sill, I moved sidewise, then turned and braced my back against the wall. With my feet against the edge of the bunk, I thrust it away with all the strength in both my legs. A creak and a ripping sound, and the bar pulled slowly out from its bolts.

But a roar and thunder of feet told me that the throng outside had gained entrance to the hall at last.

I heard a last futile flurry of protesting cries from the councilmen as the steps echoed with the charge of many heavy boots. I waited no longer, but swung myself to the sill and wriggled through the narrow space where the bar had come out. A lapel of my jacket tore against the frame, but I made it. Clinging by the other bar, I made out at my side a narrow band of perpendicular darkness against the wall, and clutched at it. It was a tin drainpipe, by the feel of it.

An attack was being made upon the door of the cell. The wood splintered before a torrent of blows, and I heard people pushing in.

"He's gone!" yelled a rough voice, and, a moment later: "Hey, look at the window!"

I had hold of the drainpipe, and gave it my entire weight. Next instant it had torn loose from its flimsy supports and bent sickeningly outward. Yet it did not let me down at once, acting rather as a slender sapling to the top of which an adventuresome boy has sprung. Still holding to it, I fell sprawling in the snow twenty feet beneath the window I had quitted. Somebody shouted from above and a gun spoke.

"Get him!" screamed many voices. "Get him, you down below!"

But I was up and running for my life. The snow-filled square seemed to whip away beneath my feet. Dodging around the war memorial, I came face to face with somebody in a bearskin coat. He shouted for me to halt, in the reedy voice of an ungrown lad, and the fierce-set face that shoved at me had surely never felt a razor. But I, who dared not be merciful even to so untried an enemy, struck with both fists even as I hurtled against him. He whimpered and dropped, and I, springing over his falling body, dashed on.

A wind was rising, and it bore to me the howls of my pursuers from the direction of the hall. Two or three more guns went off, and one bullet whickered over my head. By then I had reached the far side of the square, hurried across the street and up an alley. The snow, still falling densely, served to baffle the men who ran shouting in my wake. Too, nearly everyone who had been on the streets had gone to the front of the hall, and except for the boy at the memorial none offered to turn me back.

I came out upon a street beyond the square, quiet and ill-lit. Along this way, I remembered, I could approach the Gird home, where my automobile was parked. Once at the wheel, I could drive to the county seat and demand protection from the sheriff. But, as I came cautiously near the place and could see through the blizzard the outline of the car, I heard loud voices. A part of the mob had divined my intent and had branched off to meet me.

I ran down a side street, but they had seen me. "There he is!" they shrieked at one another. "Plug him!" Bullets struck the wall of a house as I fled past it, and the owner, springing to the door with an angry protest, joined the chase a moment later.

* * * *

I was panting and staggering by now, and so were most of my pursuers. Only three or four, lean young athletes, were gaining and coming even close to my heels. With wretched determination I maintained my pace, winning free of the close-set houses of the town, wriggling between the rails of a fence and striking off through the drifting snow of a field.

"Hey, he's heading for the Croft!" someone was wheezing, not far behind.

"Let him go in," growled another runner. "He'll wish he hadn't."

Yet again someone fired, and yet again the bullet went wide of me; moving swiftly, and half veiled by the dark and the wind-tossed snowfall, I was a bad target that night. And, lifting my head, I saw indeed the dense timber of the Devil's Croft, its tops seeming to toss and fall like the black waves of a high-pent sea.

It was an inspiration, helped by the shouts of the mob. Nobody went into that grove—avoidance of it had become a community habit, almost a community instinct. Even if my enemies paused only temporarily I could shelter well among the trunks, catch my breath, perhaps hide indefinitely. And surely Zoberg would be recovered, would back up my protest of innocence. With two words for it, the fantasy would not seem so ridiculous. All this I sorted over in my mind as I ran toward the Devil's Croft.

Another rail fence rose in my way. I feared for a moment that it would baffle me, so fast and far had I run and so greatly drained away was my strength. Yet I scrambled over somehow, slipped and fell beyond, got up and ran crookedly on. The trees were close now. Closer. Within a dozen yards. Behind me I heard oaths and warning exclamations. The pursuit was ceasing at last.

I found myself against close-set evergreens; that would be the hedge of which Susan Gird had told me. Pushing between and through the interlaced branches, I hurried on for five or six steps, cannoned from a big tree-trunk, went sprawling, lifted myself for another brief run and then, with my legs like strips of paper, dropped once more. I crept forward on hands and knees. Finally I collapsed upon my face. The weight of all I had endured—the séance, the horrible death of John Gird, my arrest, my breaking from the cell and my wild run for life—overwhelmed me as I lay.

Thus I must lie, I told myself hazily, until they came and caught me. I heard, or fancied I heard, movement near by, then a trilling whistle. A signal? It sounded like the song of a little frog. Odd thought in this blizzard. I was thinking foolishly of frogs, while I sprawled face down in the snow....

But where was the snow?

There was damp underneath, but it was warm damp, like that of a riverside in July. In my nostrils was a smell of green life, the smell of parks and hot-houses. My fists closed upon something.

Two handfuls of soft, crisp moss!

I rose to my elbows. A white flower bobbed and swayed before my nose, shedding perfume upon me.

Far away, as though in another world, I heard the rising of the wind that was beating the snow into great drifts—but that was outside the Devil's Croft.

CHAPTER 6

"EYES OF FIRE!"

It proves something for human habit and narcotic-dependence that my first action upon rising was to pull out a cigarette and light it.

The match flared briefly upon rich greenness. I might have been in a sub-tropical swamp. Then the little flame winked out and the only glow was the tip of my cigarette. I gazed upward for a glimpse of the sky, but found only darkness. Leafy branches made a roof over me. My brow felt damp. It was sweat—warm sweat.

I held the coal of the cigarette to my wrist-watch. It seemed to have stopped, and I lifted it to my ear. No ticking—undoubtedly I had jammed it into silence, perhaps at the séance, perhaps during my escape from prison and the mob. The hands pointed to eighteen minutes past eight, and it was certainly much later than that. I wished for the electric torch that I had dropped in the dining-room at Gird's, then was glad I had not brought it to flash my position to possible watchers outside the grove.

Yet the tight cedar hedge and the inner belts of trees and bushes, richly foliaged as they must be, would certainly hide me and any light I might make. I felt considerably stronger in body and will by now, and made shift to walk gropingly toward the center of the timber-clump. Once, stooping to finger the ground on which I walked, I felt not only moss but soft grass. Again, a hanging vine dragged across my face. It was wet, as if from condensed mist, and it bore sweet flowers that showed dimly like little pallid trumpets in the dark.

The frog-like chirping that I had heard when first I fell had been going on without cessation. It was much nearer now, and when I turned in its direction, I saw a little glimmer of water. Two more careful steps, and my foot sank into wet, warm mud. I stooped and put a hand into a tiny stream, almost as warm as the air. The frog, whose home I was disturbing, fell silent once more.

I struck a match, hoping to see a way across. The stream was not more than three feet in width, and it flowed slowly from the interior of the grove. In that direction hung low mists, through which broad leaves gleamed wetly. On my side its brink was fairly clear, but on the other grew lush, dripping bushes. I felt in the stream once more, and found it was little more than a finger deep. Then, holding the end of the match in my fingers, I stooped as low as possible, to see what I could of the nature of the ground beneath the bushes.

The small beam carried far, and I let myself think of Shakespeare's philosophy anent the candle and the good deed in a naughty world. Then philosophy and Shakespeare flew from my mind, for I saw beneath the bushes the feet of—of what stood behind them.

They were two in number, those feet; but not even at first glimpse did I think they were human. I had an impression of round pedestals and calfless shanks, dark and hairy. They moved as I looked, moved cautiously closer, as if their owner was equally anxious to see me. I dropped the match into the stream and sprang up and back.

No pursuer from the town would have feet like that.

My heart began to pound as it had never pounded during my race for life. I clutched at the low limb of a tree, hoping to tear it loose for a possible weapon of defense; the wood was rotten, and almost crumpled in my grasp.

"Who's there?" I challenged, but most unsteadily and without much menace in my voice. For answer the bushes rustled yet again, and something blacker than they showed itself among them.

I cannot be ashamed to say that I retreated again, farther this time; let him who has had a like experience decide whether to blame me. Feeling my way among the trees, I put several stout stems between me and that lurker by the water-side. They would not fence it off, but might baffle it for a moment. Meanwhile, I heard the water splash. It was wading cautiously through—it was going to follow me.

I found myself standing in a sort of lane, and did not bother until later to wonder how a lane could exist in that grove where no man ever walked. It was a welcome avenue of flight to me, and I went along it at a swift, crouching run. The footing, as everywhere, was damp and mossy, and I made very little noise. Not so my unchancy companion of the brook, for I heard a heavy body crashing among twigs and branches to one side. I began to ask myself, as I hurried, what the beast could be—for I was sure that it was a beast. A dog from some farmhouse, that did not know or understand the law against entering the Devil's Croft? That I had seen only two feet did not preclude two more, I now assured myself, and I would have welcomed a big, friendly dog. Yet I did not know that this one was friendly, and could not bid myself to stop and see.

The lane wound suddenly to the right, and then into a clearing.

Here, too, the branches overhead kept out the snow and the light, but things were visible ever so slightly. I stood as if in a room, earth-floored, trunk-walled, leaf-thatched. And I paused for a breath—it was more damply warm than ever. With that breath came some strange new serenity of spirit, even an amused self-mockery. What had I seen and heard, indeed? I had come into the grove after a terrific hour or so of danger and exertion, and my mind had at once busied itself in building grotesque dangers where no dangers could be. Have another smoke, I said to myself, and get hold of your imagination; already that pursuit-noise you fancied has gone. Alone in the clearing and the dark, I smiled as though to mock myself back into self-confidence. Even this little patch of summer night into which I had blundered from the heart of the blizzard—even it had some good and probably simple explanation. I fished out a cigarette and struck a light.

At that moment I was facing the bosky tunnel from which I had emerged into the open space. My matchlight struck two sparks in that tunnel, two sparks that were pushing stealthily toward me. Eyes of fire!

Cigarette and match fell from my hands. For one wild half-instant I thought of flight, then knew with a throat-stopping certainty that I must not turn my back on this thing. I planted my feet and clenched my fists.

"Who's there?" I cried, as once before at the side of the brook.

This time I had an answer. It was a hoarse, deep-chested rumble, it might have been a growl or an oath. And a shadow stole out from the lane, straightening up almost within reach of me.

I had seen that silhouette before, misshapen and point-eared, in the dining-room of John Gird.

CHAPTER 7

"HAD THE THING BEEN SO HAIRY?"

It did not charge at once, or I might have been killed then, like John Gird, and the writing of this account left to another hand. While it closed cautiously in, I was able to set myself for defense. I also made out some of its details, and hysterically imagined more.

Its hunched back and narrow shoulders gave nothing of weakness to its appearance, suggesting rather an inhuman plenitude of bone and muscle behind. At first it was crouched, as if on all-fours, but then it reared. For all its legs were bent, its great length of body made it considerably taller than I. Upper limbs—I hesitate at calling them arms—sparred questingly at me.

I moved a stride backward, but kept my face to the enemy.

"You killed Gird!" I accused it, in a voice steady enough but rather strained and shrill. "Come on and kill me! I promise you a damned hard bargain of it."

The creature shrank away in turn, as though it understood the words and was momentarily daunted by them. Its head, which I could not make out, sank low before those crooked shoulders and swayed rhythmically like the head of a snake before striking. The rush was coming, and I knew it.

"Come on!" I dared it again. "What are you waiting for? I'm not chained down, like Gird. I'll give you a devil of a fight."

I had my fists up and I feinted, boxer-wise, with a little weaving jerk of the knees. The blot of blackness started violently, ripped out a snarl from somewhere inside it, and sprang at me.

I had an impression of paws flung out and a head twisted sidewise, with long teeth bared to snap at my throat. Probably it meant to clutch my shoulders with its fingers—it had them, I had felt them on my knee at the séance. But I had planned my own campaign in those tense seconds. I slid my left foot forward as the enemy lunged, and my left fist drove for the muzzle. My knuckles barked against the huge, inhuman teeth, and I brought over a roundabout right, with shoulder and hip driving in back of it. The head, slanted as it was, received this right fist high on the brow. I felt the impact of solid bone, and the body floundered away to my left. I broke ground right, turned and raised my hands as before.

"Want any more of the same?" I taunted it, as I would a human antagonist after scoring.

The failure of its attack had been only temporary. My blows had set it off balance, but could hardly have been decisive. I heard a coughing snort, as though the thing's muzzle was bruised, and it quartered around toward me once more. Without warning and with amazing speed it rushed.

I had no time to set myself now. I did try to leap backward, but I was not quick enough. It had me; gripping the lapels of my coat and driving me down and over with its flying weight. I felt the wet ground spin under my heels, and then it came flying up against my shoulders. Instinctively I had clutched upward at a throat with my right hand, clutched a handful of skin, loose and rankly shaggy. My left, also by instinct, flew backward to break my fall. It closed on something hard, round and smooth.

The rank odor that I had known at the séance was falling around me like a blanket, and the clashing white teeth shoved nearer, nearer. But the rock in my left hand spelled sudden hope. Without trying to roll out from under, I smote with that rock. My clutch on the hairy throat helped me to judge accurately where the head would be. A moment later, and the struggling bulk above me went limp under the impact. Shoving it aside, I scrambled free and gained my feet once more.

The monster lay motionless where I had thrust it from me. Every nerve a-tingle, I stooped. My hand poised the rock for another smashing blow, but there was no sign of fight from the fallen shape. I could hear only a gusty breathing, as of something in stunned pain.

"Lie right where you are, you murdering brute," I cautioned it, my voice ringing exultant as I realized I had won. "If you move, I'll smash your skull in."

My right hand groped in my pocket for a match, struck it on the back of my leg. I bent still closer for a clear look at my enemy.

Had the thing been so hairy? Now, as I gazed, it seemed only sparsely furred. The ears, too, were blunter than I thought, and the muzzle not so—

Why, it was half human! Even as I watched, it was becoming more human still, a sprawled human figure! And, as the fur seemed to vanish in patches, was it clothing I saw, as though through the rents in a bearskin overcoat?

My senses churned in my own head. The fear that had ridden me all night became suddenly unreasoning. I fled as before, this time without a thought of where I was going or what I would do. The forbidden grove, lately so welcome as a refuge, swarmed with evil. I reached the edge of the clearing, glanced back once. The thing I had stricken down was beginning to stir, to get up. I ran from it as from a devil.

Somehow I had come to the stream again, or to another like it. The current moved more swiftly at this point, with a noticeable murmur. As I tried to spring across I landed short, and gasped in sudden pain, for the water was scalding hot. Of such are the waters of hell....

* * * *

I cannot remember my flight through that steaming swamp that might have been a corner of Satan's own park. Somewhere along the way I found a tough, fleshy stem, small enough to rend from its rooting and wield as a club. With it in my hand I paused, with a rather foolish desire to return along my line of retreat for another and decisive encounter with the shaggy being. But what if it would foresee my coming and lie in wait? I knew how swiftly it could spring, how strong was its grasp. Once at close quarters, my club would be useless, and those teeth might find their objective. I cast aside the impulse, that had welled from I know not what primitive core of me, and hurried on.

Evergreens were before me on a sudden, and through them filtered a blast of cold air. The edge of the grove, and beyond it the snow and the open sky, perhaps a resumption of the hunt by the mob; but capture and death at their hands would be clean and welcome compared to—

Feet squelched in the dampness behind me.

I pivoted with a hysterical oath, and swung up my club in readiness to strike. The great dark outline that had come upon me took one step closer, then paused. I sprang at it, struck and missed as it dodged to one side.

"All right then, let's have it out," I managed to blurt, though my voice was drying up in my throat. "Come on, show your face."

"I'm not here to fight you," a good-natured voice assured me. "Why, I seldom even argue, except with proven friends."

I relaxed a trifle, but did not lower my club. "Who are you?"

"Judge Keith Pursuivant," was the level response, as though I had not just finished trying to kill him. "You must be the young man they're so anxious to hang, back in town. Is that right?"

I made no answer.

"Silence makes admission," the stranger said. "Well, come along to my house. This grove is between it and town, and nobody will bother us for the night, at least."

CHAPTER 8

"A TRICK THAT ALMOST KILLED YOU."

When I stepped into the open with Judge Keith Pursuivant, the snow had ceased and a full moon glared through a rip in the clouds, making diamond dust of the sugary drifts. By its light I saw my companion with some degree of plainness—a man of great height and girth, with a wide black hat and a voluminous gray ulster. His face was as round as the moon itself, at least as shiny, and much warmer to look at. A broad bulbous nose and broad bulbous eyes beamed at me, while under a drooping blond mustache a smile seemed to be lurking. Apparently he considered the situation a pleasant one.

"I'm not one of the mob," he informed me reassuringly. "These pastimes of the town do not attract me. I left such things behind when I dropped out of politics and practise—oh, I was active in such things, ten years ago up North—and took up meditation."

"I've heard that you keep to yourself," I told him.

"You heard correctly. My black servant does the shopping and brings me the gossip. Most of the time it bores me, but not today, when I learned about you and the killing of John Gird—"

"And you came looking for me?"

"Of course. By the way, that was a wise impulse, ducking into the Devil's Croft."

But I shuddered, and not with the chill of the outer night. He made a motion for me to come along, and we began tramping through the soft snow toward a distant light under the shadow of a hill. Meanwhile I told him something of my recent adventures, saving for the last my struggle with the monster in the grove.

He heard me through, whistling through his teeth at various points. At the end of my narrative he muttered to himself:

"The hairy ones shall dance—"

"What was that, sir?" I broke in, without much courtesy.

"I was quoting from the prophet Isaiah. He was speaking of ruined Babylon, not a strange transplanted bit of the tropics, but otherwise it falls pat. Suggestive of a demon-festival. 'The hairy ones shall dance there.'"

"Isaiah, you say? I used to be something of a Bible reader, but I'm afraid I don't remember the passage."

He smiled sidewise at me. "But I'm translating direct from the original, Mr.—Wills is the name, eh? The original Hebrew of the prophet Isaiah, whoever he was. The classic-ridden compilers of the King James Version have satyrs dancing, and the prosaic Revised Version offers nothing more startling than goats. But Isaiah and the rest of the ancient peoples knew that there were 'hairy ones.' Perhaps you encountered one of that interesting breed tonight."

"I don't want to encounter it a second time," I confessed, and again I shuddered.

"That is something we will talk over more fully. What do you think of the Turkish bath accommodations you have just left behind?"

"To tell you the truth, I don't know what to think. Growing green stuff and a tropical temperature, with snow outside—"

He waved the riddle away. "Easily and disappointingly explained, Mr. Wills. Hot springs."

I stopped still, shin-deep in wet snow. "What!" I ejaculated.

"Oh, I've been there many times, in defiance of local custom and law—I'm not a native, you see." Once more his warming smile. "There are at least three springs, and the thick growth of trees makes a natural enclosure, roof and walls, to hold in the damp heat. It's not the only place of its kind in the world, Mr.

Wills. But the thing you met there is a trifle more difficult of explanation. Come on home—we'll both feel better when we sit down."

* * * *

We finished the journey in half an hour. Judge Pursuivant's house was stoutly made of heavy hewn timbers, somewhat resembling certain lodges I had seen in England. Inside was a large, low-ceilinged room with a hanging oil lamp and a welcome open fire. A fat blond cat came leisurely forward to greet us. Its broad, good-humored face, large eyes and drooping whiskers gave it somewhat of a resemblance to its master.

"Better get your things off," advised the judge. He raised his voice. "William!"

A squat negro with a sensitive brown face appeared from a door at the back of the house.

"Bring in a bathrobe and slippers for this gentleman," ordered Judge Pursuivant, and himself assisted me to take off my muddy jacket. Thankfully I peeled off my other garments, and when the servant appeared with the robe I slid into it with a sigh.

"I'm in your hands, Judge Pursuivant," I said. "If you want to turn me over—"

"I might surrender you to an officer," he interrupted, "but never to a lawless mob. You'd better sit here for a time—and talk to me."

Near the fire was a desk, with an arm-chair at either side of it. We took seats, and when William returned from disposing of my wet clothes, he brought along a tray with a bottle of whisky, a siphon and some glasses. The judge prepared two drinks and handed one to me. At his insistence, I talked for some time about the séance and the events leading up to it.

"Remarkable," mused Judge Pursuivant. Then his great shrewd eyes studied me. "Don't go to sleep there, Mr. Wills. I know you're tired, but I want to talk lycanthropy."

"Lycanthropy?" I repeated. "You mean the science of the werewolf?" I smiled and shook my head. "I'm afraid I'm no authority, sir. Anyway, this was no witchcraft—it was a bona fide spirit séance, with ectoplasm."

"Hum!" snorted the judge. "Witchcraft, spiritism! Did it ever occur to you that they might be one and the same thing?"

"Inasmuch as I never believed in either of them, it never did occur to me."

Judge Pursuivant finished his drink and wiped his mustache. "Skepticism does not become you too well, Mr. Wills, if you will pardon my frankness. In any case, you saw something very werewolfish indeed, not an hour ago. Isn't that the truth?"

"It was some kind of a trick," I insisted stubbornly.

"A trick that almost killed you and made you run for your life?"

I shook my head. "I know I saw the thing," I admitted. "I even felt it." My eyes dropped to the bruised knuckles of my right hand. "Yet I was fooled—as a magician, I know all about fooling. There can be no such thing as a werewolf."

"Have a drink," coaxed Judge Pursuivant, exactly as if I had had none yet. With big, deft hands he poured whisky, then soda, into my glass and gave the mixture a stirring shake. "Now then," he continued, sitting back in his chair once more, "the time has come to speak of many things."

He paused, and I, gazing over the rim of that welcome glass, thought how much he looked like a rosy blond walrus.

"I'm going to show you," he announced, "that a man can turn into a beast, and back again."

CHAPTER 9

"TO A TERRIFIED VICTIM
HE IS DOOM ITSELF."

He leaned toward the bookshelf beside him, pawed for a moment, then laid two sizable volumes on the desk between us.

"If this were a fantasy tale, Mr. Wills," he said with a hint of one of his smiles, "I would place before you an unthinkably rare book—one that offered, in terms too brilliant and compelling for argument, the awful secrets of the universe, past, present and to come."

He paused to polish a pair of pince-nez and to clamp them upon the bridge of his broad nose.

"However," he resumed, "this is reality, sober if uneasy. And I give you, not some forgotten grimoire out of the mystic past, but two works by two recognized and familiar authorities."

I eyed the books. "May I see?"

For answer he thrust one of them, some six hundred pages in dark blue cloth, across the desk and into my hands. "*Thirty Years of Psychical Research*, by the late Charles Richet, French master in the spirit-investigation field," he informed me. "Faithfully and interestingly translated by Stanley De Brath. Published here in America, in 1923."

I took the book and opened it. "I knew Professor Richet, slightly. Years ago, when I was just beginning this sort of thing, I was entertained by him in London. He introduced me to Conan Doyle."

"Then you're probably familiar with his book. Yes? Well, the other," and he took up the second volume, almost as large as the Richet and bound in light buff, "is by Montague Summers, whom I call the premier demonologist of today. He's gathered all the lycanthropy-lore available."

I had read Mr. Summers' *Geography of Witchcraft* and his two essays on the vampire, and I made bold to say so.

"This is a companion volume to them," Judge Pursuivant told me, opening the book. "It is called *The Werewolf.*" He scrutinized the flyleaf. "Published in 1934—thoroughly modern, you see. Here's a bit of Latin, Mr. Wills: *Intrabunt lupi rapaces in vos, non parcentes gregi.*"

I crinkled my brow in the effort to recall my high school Latin, then began slowly to translate, a word at a time: "'Enter hungry wolves—'"

"Save that scholarship," Judge Pursuivant broke in. "It's more early Scripture, though not so early as the bit about the hairy ones—vulgate for a passage from the Acts of the Apostles, twentieth chapter, twenty-ninth verse. 'Ravenous wolves shall enter among you, not sparing the flock.' Apparently that disturbing possibility exists even today."

He leafed through the book. "Do you know," he asked, "that Summers gives literally dozens of instances of lycanthropy, things that are positively known to have happened?"

I took another sip of whisky and water. "Those are only legends, surely."

"They are nothing of the sort!" The judge's eyes protruded even more in his earnestness, and he tapped the pages with an excited forefinger. "There are four excellent cases listed in his chapter on France alone—sworn to, tried and sentenced by courts—"

"But weren't they during the Middle Ages?" I suggested.

He shook his great head. "No, during the Sixteenth Century, the peak of the Renaissance. Oh, don't smile at the age, Mr. Wills. It produced Shakespeare, Bacon, Montaigne, Galileo, Leonardo, Martin Luther; Descartes and Spinoza were its legitimate children, and Voltaire builded upon it. Yet werewolves were known, seen, convicted—"

"Convicted on what grounds?" I interrupted quickly, for I was beginning to reflect his warmth.

For answer he turned more pages. "Here is the full account of the case of Stubbe Peter, or Peter Stumpf," he said. "A contemporary record, telling of Stumpf's career in and out of wolf-form, his capture in the very act of shifting shape, his confession and execution—all near Cologne in the year 1589. Listen."

He read aloud: "'Witnesses that this is true. Tyse Artyne. William Brewar. Adolf Staedt. George Bores. With divers others that have seen the same.'" Slamming the book shut, he looked up at me, the twinkle coming back into his spectacled eyes. "Well, Mr. Wills? How do those names sound to you?"

"Why, like the names of honest German citizens."

"Exactly. Honest, respectable, solid. And their testimony is hard to pass off with a laugh, even at this distance in time, eh?"

He had almost made me see those witnesses, leather-jerkined and broad-breeched, with heavy jaws and squinting eyes, taking their turn at the quill pen with which they set their names to that bizarre document. "With divers others that have seen the same"—perhaps too frightened to hold pen or make signature....

"Still," I said slowly, "Germany of the Renaissance, the Sixteenth Century; and there have been so many changes since."

"Werewolves have gone out of fashion, you mean? Ah, you admit that they might have existed." He fairly beamed his triumph. "So have beards gone out of fashion, but they will sprout again if we lay down our razors. Let's go at it another way. Let's talk about materialization—ectoplasm—for the moment." He relaxed, and across his great girth his fingertips sought one another. "Suppose you explain, briefly and simply, what ectoplasm is considered to be."

I was turning toward the back of Richet's book. "It's in here, Judge Pursuivant. To be brief and simple, as you say, certain mediums apparently exude an unclassified material called ectoplasm. This, at first light and vaporescent, becomes firm and takes shape, either upon the body of the medium or as a separate and living creature."

"And you don't believe in this phenomenon?" he prompted, with something of insistence.

"I have never said that I didn't," I replied truthfully, "even before my experience of this evening went so far toward convincing me. But, with the examples I have seen, I felt that true scientific control was lacking. With all their science, most of the investigators trust too greatly."

Judge Pursuivant shook with gentle laughter. "They are doctors for the most part, and this honesty of theirs is a professional failing that makes them look for it in others. You—begging your pardon—are a magician, a professional deceiver, and you expect trickery in all whom you meet. Perhaps a good lawyer with trial experience, with a level head and a sense of competent material evidence for both sides, should attend these séances, eh?"

"You're quite right," I said heartily.

"But, returning to the subject, what else can be said about ectoplasm? That is, if it actually exists."

I had found in Richet's book the passage for which I had been searching. "It says here that bits of ectoplasm have been secured in rare instances, and that some of these have been examined microscopically. There were traces of fatty tissue, bacterial forms and epithelium."

"Ah! Those were the findings of Schrenck-Notzing. A sound man and a brilliant one, hard to corrupt or fool. It makes ectoplasm sound organic, does it not?"

* * * *

I nodded agreement, and my head felt heavy, as if full of sober and important matters. "As for me," I went on, "I never have had much chance to examine the stuff. Whenever I get hold of an ectoplasmic hand, it melts like butter."

"They generally do," the judge commented, "or so the reports say. Yet they themselves are firm and strong when they touch or seize."

"Right, sir."

"It's when attacked, or even frightened, as with a camera flashlight, that the ectoplasm vanishes or is reabsorbed?" he prompted further.

"So Richet says here," I agreed once more, "and so I have found."

"Very good. Now," and his manner took on a flavor of the legal, "I shall sum up: Ectoplasm is put forth by certain spirit mediums, who are mysteriously adapted for it, under favorable conditions that include darkness, quiet, self-confidence. It takes form, altering the appearance of the medium or making up a separate body. It is firm and strong, but vanishes when attacked or frightened. Right so far, eh?"

"Right," I approved.

"Now, for the word *medium* substitute *wizard*." His grin burst out again, and he began to mix a third round of drinks. "A wizard, having darkness and quiet and being disposed to change shape, exudes a material that gives him a new shape and character. Maybe it is bestial, to match a fierce or desperate spirit within. There may be a shaggy pelt, a sharp muzzle, taloned paws and rending fangs. To a terrified victim he is doom itself. But to a brave adversary, facing and fighting him—"

He flipped his way through Summers' book, as I had with Richet's. "Listen: '...the shape of the werewolf will be removed if he be reproached by name as a werewolf, or if again he be thrice addressed by his Christian name, or struck three blows on the forehead with a knife, or that three drops of blood should be drawn.' Do you see the parallels, man? Shouted at, bravely denounced, or slightly wounded, his false beast-substance fades from him." He flung out his hands, as though appealing to a jury. "I marvel nobody ever thought of it before."

"But nothing so contrary to nature has a natural explanation," I objected, and very idiotic the phrase sounded in my own ears.

He laughed, and I could not blame him. "I'll confound you with another of your own recent experiences. What could seem more contrary to nature than the warmth and greenness of the inside of Devil's Croft? And what is more simply natural than the hot springs that make it possible?"

"Yet, an envelope of bestiality, beast-muzzle on human face, beast-paws on human hands—"

"I can support that by more werewolf-lore. I don't even have to open Summers, everyone has heard the story. A wolf attacks a traveler, who with his sword lops off a paw. The beast howls and flees, and the paw it leaves behind is a human hand."

"That's an old one, in every language."

"Probably because it happened so often. There's your human hand, with the beast-paw forming upon and around it, then vanishing like wounded ectoplasm. Where's the weak point, Wills? Name it, I challenge you."

I felt the glass shake in my hand, and a chilly wind brushed my spine. "There's one point," I made myself say. "You may think it a slender one, even a quibble. But ectoplasms make human forms, not animal."

"How do you know they don't make animal forms?" Judge Pursuivant crowed, leaning forward across the deck. "Because, of the few you've seen and disbelieved, only human faces and bodies showed? My reply is there in your hands. Open Richet's book to page 545, Mr. Wills. Page 545 … got it? Now, the passage I marked, about the medium Burgik. Read it aloud."

He sank back into his chair once more, waiting in manifest delight. I found the place, underscored with pencil, and my voice was hoarse as I obediently read:

"'My trouser leg was strongly pulled and a strange, ill-defined form that seemed to have paws like those of a dog or small monkey climbed on my knee. I could feel its weight, very light, and something like the muzzle of an animal touched my cheek.'"

"There you are, Wills," Judge Pursuivant was crying. "Notice that it happened in Warsaw, close to the heart of the werewolf country. Hmmm, reading that passage made you sweat a bit—remembering what you saw in the Devil's Croft, eh?"

I flung down the book.

"You've done much toward convincing me," I admitted. "I'd rather have the superstitious peasant's belief, though, the one I've always scoffed at."

"Rationalizing the business didn't help, then? It did when I explained the Devil's Croft and the springs."

"But the springs don't chase you with sharp teeth. And, as I was saying, the peasant had a protection that the scientist lacks—trust in his crucifix and his Bible."

"Why shouldn't he have that trust, and why shouldn't you?" Again the judge was rummaging in his book-case. "Those symbols of faith gave him what is needed, a strong heart to drive back the menace, whether it be wolf-demon or ectoplasmic bogy. Here, my friend."

He laid a third book on the desk. It was a Bible, red-edged and leather-backed, worn from much use.

"Have a read at that while you finish your drink," he advised me. "*The Gospel According to St. John* is good, and it's already marked. Play you're a peasant, hunting for comfort."

Like a dutiful child I opened the Bible to where a faded purple ribbon lay between the pages. But already Judge Pursuivant was quoting from memory:

"'In the beginning was the Word, and the Word was with God, and the Word was God. The same was in the beginning with God. All things were made by him; and without him was not anything made that was made....'"

CHAPTER 10

"BLOOD-LUST AND COMPASSION."

It may seem incredible that later in the night I slept like a dead pig; yet I had reason.

First of all there was the weariness that had followed my dangers and exertions; then Judge Pursuivant's whisky and logic combined to reassure me; finally, the leather couch in his study, its surface comfortably hollowed by much reclining thereon, was a sedative in itself. He gave me two quilts, very warm and very light, and left me alone. I did not stir until a rattle of breakfast dishes awakened me.

William, the judge's servant, had carefully brushed my clothes. My shoes also showed free of mud, though they still felt damp and clammy. The judge himself furnished me with a clean shirt and socks, both items very loose upon me, and lent me his razor.

"Some friends of yours called during the night," he told me dryly.

"Friends?"

"Yes, from the town. Five of them, with ropes and guns. They announced very definitely that they intended to decorate the flagpole in the public square with your corpse. There was also some informal talk about drinking your blood. We may have vampires as well as werewolves hereabouts."

I almost cut my lip with the razor. "How did you get rid of them?" I asked quickly. "They must have followed my tracks."

"Lucky there was more snow after we got in," he replied, "and they came here only as a routine check-up. They must have visited every house within miles. Oh, turning them away was easy. I feigned wild enthusiasm for the manhunt, and asked if I couldn't come along."

He smiled reminiscently, his mustache stirring like a rather genial blond snake.

"Then what?" I prompted him, dabbing on more lather.

"Why, they were delighted. I took a rifle and spent a few hours on the trail. You weren't to be found at all, so we returned to town. Excitement reigns there, you can believe."

"What kind of excitement?"

"Blood-lust and compassion. Since Constable O'Bryant is wounded, his younger brother, a strong advocate of your immediate capture and execution, is serving as a volunteer guardian of the peace. He's acting on an old appointment by his brother as deputy, to serve without pay. He told the council—a badly scared group—that he has sent for help to the county seat, but I am sure he did nothing of the kind. Meanwhile, the Croft is surrounded by scouts, who hope to catch you sneaking out of it. And the women of the town are looking after Susan Gird and your friend, the *Herr Doktor*."

I had finished shaving. "How is Doctor Zoberg?" I inquired through the towel.

"Still pretty badly shaken up. I tried to get in and see him, but it was impossible. I understand he went out for a while, early in the evening, but almost collapsed. Just now he is completely surrounded by cooing old ladies with soup and herb tea. Miss Gird was feeling much better, and talked to me for a while. I'm not really on warm terms with the town, you know; people think it's indecent for me to live out here alone and not give them a chance to gossip about me. So I was pleasurably surprized to get a kind word from Miss Susan. She told me, very softly for fear someone might overhear, that she hopes you aren't caught. She is sure that you did not kill her father."

We went into his dining-room, where William offered pancakes, fried bacon and the strongest black coffee I ever tasted.

In the midst of it all, I put down my fork and faced the judge suddenly. He grinned above his cup.

"Well, Mr. Wills? 'Stung by the splendor of a sudden thought'—all you need is a sensitive hand clasped to your inspired brow."

"You said," I reminded him, "that Susan Gird is sure that I didn't kill her father."

"So I did."

"She told you that herself. She also seemed calm, self-contained, instead of in mourning for—"

"Oh, come, come!" He paused to shift a full half-dozen cakes to his plate and skilfully drenched them with syrup. "That's rather ungrateful of you, Mr. Wills, suspecting her of parricide."

"Did I say that?" I protested, feeling my ears turning bright red.

"You would have if I hadn't broken your sentence in the middle," he accused, and put a generous portion of pancake into his mouth. As he chewed he twinkled at me through his pince-nez, and I felt unaccountably foolish.

"If Susan Gird had truly killed her father," he resumed, after swallowing, "she would be more adroitly theatrical. She would weep, swear vengeance on his murderer, and be glad to hear that someone else had been accused of the crime. She would even invent details to help incriminate that someone else."

"Perhaps she doesn't know that she killed him," I offered.

"Perhaps not. You mean that a new mind, as well as a new body, may invest the werewolf—or ectoplasmic medium—at time of change."

I jerked my head in agreement.

"Then Susan Gird, as she is normally, must be innocent. Come, Mr. Wills! Would you blame poor old Doctor Jekyll for the crimes of his *alter ego*, Mr. Hyde?"

"I wouldn't want to live in the same house with Doctor Jekyll."

Judge Pursuivant burst into a roar of laughter, at which William, bringing fresh supplies from the kitchen, almost dropped his tray. "So romance enters the field of psychic research!" the judge crowed at me.

I stiffened, outraged. "Judge Pursuivant, I certainly did not—"

"I know, you didn't say it, but again I anticipated you. So it's not the thought of her possible unconscious crime, but the chance of comfortable companionship that perplexes you." He stopped laughing suddenly. "I'm sorry, Wills. Forgive me. I shouldn't laugh at this, or indeed at any aspect of the whole very serious business."

I could hardly take real offense at the man who had rescued and sheltered me, and I said so. We finished breakfast, and he sought his overcoat and wide hat.

"I'm off for town again," he announced. "There are one or two points to be settled there, for your safety and my satisfaction. Do you mind being left alone? There's an interesting lot of books in my study. You might like to look at a copy of Dom Calmet's *Dissertations*, if you read French; also a rather slovenly *Wicked Bible*, signed by Pierre De Lancre. J. W. Wickwar, the witchcraft authority, thinks that such a thing does not exist, but I know of two others. Or, if you feel that you're having enough of demonology in real life, you will find a whole row of light novels, including most of P. G. Wodehouse." He held out his hand in farewell. "William will get you anything you want. There's tobacco and a choice of pipes on my desk. Whisky, too, though you don't look like the sort that drinks before noon."

With that he was gone, and I watched him from the window. He moved sturdily across the bright snow to a shed, slid open its door and entered. Soon there emerged a sedan, old but well-kept, with the judge at the wheel. He drove away down a snow-filled road toward town.

I did not know what to envy most in him, his learning, his assurance or his good-nature. The assurance, I decided once;

then it occurred to me that he was in nothing like the awkward position I held. He was only a sympathetic ally—but why was he that, even? I tried to analyze his motives, and could not.

* * * *

Sitting down in his study, I saw on the desk the Montague Summers book on werewolves. It lay open at page 111, and my eyes lighted at once upon a passage underscored in ink—apparently some time ago, for the mark was beginning to rust a trifle. It included a quotation from *Restitution of Decayed Intelligence*, written by Richard Rowlands in 1605:

> "...*werewolves* are certaine sorcerers, who hauvin annoynted their bodyes, with an oyntment which they make by the instinct of the deuil; and putting on a certain inchanted girdel, do not only vnto the view of others seeme as wolues, but to their own thinking haue both the shape and the nature of wolues, so long as they weare the said girdel. And they do dispose theselves as uery wolues, in wurrying and killing, and moste of humaine creatures."

This came to the bottom of the page, where someone, undoubtedly Pursuivant, had written: "Ointment and girdle sound as if they might have a scientific explanation." And, in the same script, but smaller, the following notes filled the margin beside:

Possible Werewolf Motivations

I. *Involuntary lycanthropy.*

    1. Must have blood to drink (connection with vampirism?).

    2. Must have secrecy.

    3. Driven to desperation by contemplating horror of own position.

II. *Voluntary lycanthropy.*

    1. Will to do evil.

    2. Will to exert power through fear.

III. *Contributing factors to becoming werewolf.*
    1. Loneliness and dissatisfaction.
    2. Hunger for forbidden foods (human flesh, etc.).
    3. Scorn and hate of fellow men, general or specific.
    4. Occult curiosity.
    5. Simon-pure insanity (Satanist complex).

Are any or all of these traits to be found in werewolf?
Find one and ask it.

* * * *

That was quite enough lycanthropy for the present, so far as I was concerned. I drew a book of Mark Twain from the shelf— I seem to remember it as *Tom Sawyer Abroad*—and read all the morning. Noon came, and I was about to ask the judge's negro servant for some lunch, when he appeared in the door of the study.

"Someone with a message, sah," he announced, and drew aside to admit Susan Gird.

I fairly sprang to my feet, dropping my book upon the desk. She advanced slowly into the room, her pale face grave but friendly. I saw that her eyes were darkly circled, and that her cheeks showed gaunt, as if with strain and weariness. She put out a hand, and I took it.

"A message?" I repeated William's words.

"Why, yes." She achieved a smile, and I was glad to see it, for both our sakes. "Judge Pursuivant got me to one side and said for me to come here. You and I are to talk the thing over."

"You mean, last night?" She nodded, and I asked further, "How did you get here?"

"Your car. I don't drive very well, but I managed."

I asked her to sit down and talk.

She told me that she remembered being in the parlor, with Constable O'Bryant questioning me. At the time she had had difficulty remembering even the beginning of the séance, and it was not until I had been taken away that she came to realize what had happened to her father. That, of course, distressed and distracted her further, and even now the whole experience was wretchedly hazy to her.

"I do recall sitting down with you," she said finally, after I had urged her for the twentieth time to think hard. "You chained me, yes, and Doctor Zoberg. Then yourself. Finally I seemed to float away, as if in a dream. I'm not even sure about how long it was."

"Had the light been out very long?" I asked craftily.

"The light out?" she echoed, patently mystified. "Oh, of course. The light was turned out, naturally. I don't remember, but I suppose you attended to that."

"I asked to try you," I confessed. "I didn't touch the lamp until after you had seemed to drop off to sleep."

She did recall to memory her father's protest at his manacles, and Doctor Zoberg's gentle inquiry if she were ready. That was all.

"How is Doctor Zoberg?" I asked her.

"Not very well, I'm afraid. He was exhausted by the experience, of course, and for a time seemed ready to break down. When the trouble began about you—the crowd gathered at the town hall—he gathered his strength and went out, to see if he could help defend or rescue you. He was gone about an hour and then he returned, bruised about the face. Somebody of the mob had handled him roughly, I think. He's resting at our place now, with a hot compress on his eye."

"Good man!" I applauded. "At least he did his best for me."

She was not finding much pleasure in her memories, however, and I suggested a change of the subject. We had lunch together, egg sandwiches and coffee, then played several hands of casino. Tiring of that, we turned to the books and she read aloud to me from Keats. Never has *The Eve of St. Agnes* sounded better to me. Evening fell, and we were preparing to take yet another meal—a meat pie, which William assured us was one of his culinary triumphs—when the door burst open and Judge Pursuivant came in.

"You've been together all the time?" he asked us at once.

"Why, yes," I said.

"Is that correct, Miss Susan? You've been in the house, every minute?"

"That is right," she seconded me.

"Then," said the judge. "You two are cleared, at least."

He paused, looking from Susan's questioning face to mine, then went on:

"That rending beast-thing in the Croft got another victim, not more than half an hour ago. O'Bryant was feeling better, ready to get back on duty. His deputy-brother, anxious to get hold of Wills first, for glory or vengeance, ventured into the place, just at dusk. He came out in a little while, torn and bitten almost to pieces, and died as he broke clear of the cedar hedge."

CHAPTER 11

"TO MEET THAT MONSTER FACE TO FACE!"

I think that both Susan and I fairly reeled before this news, like actors registering surprize in an old-fashioned melodrama. As for Judge Pursuivant, he turned to the table, cut a generous wedge of the meat pie and set it, all savory and steaming, on a plate for himself. His calm zest for the good food gave us others steadiness again, so that we sat down and even ate a little as he described his day in town.

He had found opportunity to talk to Susan in private, confiding in her about me and finally sending her to me; this, as he said, so that we would convince each other of our respective innocences. It was purely an inspiration, for he had had no idea, of course, that such conviction would turn out so final. Thereafter he made shift to enter the Gird house and talk to Doctor Zoberg.

That worthy he found sitting somewhat limply in the parlor, with John Gird's coffin in the next room. Zoberg, the judge reported, was mystified about the murder and anxious to bring to justice the townsfolk—there were more than one, it seemed—who had beaten him. Most of all, however, he was concerned about the charges against me.

"His greatest anxiety is to prove you innocent," Judge Pursuivant informed me. "He intends to bring the best lawyer possible for your defense, is willing even to assist in paying the fee. He also swears that character witnesses can be brought to testify that you are the most peaceable and law-abiding man in the country."

"That's mighty decent of him," I said. "According to your reasoning of this morning, his attitude proves him innocent, too."

"What reasoning was that?" asked Susan, and I was glad that the judge continued without answering her.

"I was glad that I had sent Miss Susan on. If your car had remained there, Mr. Wills, Doctor Zoberg might have driven off in it to rally your defenses."

"Not if I know him," I objected. "The whole business, what of the mystery and occult significances, will hold him right on the spot. He's relentlessly curious and, despite his temporary collapse, he's no coward."

"I agree with that," chimed in Susan.

As for my pursuers of the previous night, the judge went on, they had been roaming the snow-covered streets in twos and threes, heavily armed for the most part and still determined to punish me for killing their neighbor. The council was too frightened or too perplexed to deal with the situation, and the constable was still in bed, with his brother assuming authority, when Judge Pursuivant made his inquiries. The judge went to see the wounded man, who very pluckily determined to rise and take up his duties again.

"I'll arrest the man who plugged me," O'Bryant had promised grimly, "and that kid brother of mine can quit playing policeman."

The judge applauded these sentiments, and brought him hot food and whisky, which further braced his spirits. In the evening came the invasion by the younger O'Bryant of the Devil's Croft, and his resultant death at the claws and teeth of what prowled there.

"His throat was so torn open and filled with blood that he could not speak," the judge concluded, "but he pointed back into the timber, and then tried to trace something in the snow with his finger. It looked like a wolf's head, with pointed nose and ears. He died before he finished."

"You saw him come out?" I asked.

"No. I'd gone back to town, but later I saw the body, and the sketch in the snow."

He finished his dinner and pushed back his chair. "Now," he said heartily, "it's up to us."

"Up to us to do what?" I inquired.

"To meet that monster face to face," he replied. "There are three of us and, so far as I can ascertain, but one of the enemy." Both Susan and I started to speak, but he held up his hand, smiling. "I know without being reminded that the odds are still against us, because the one enemy is fierce and blood-drinking, and can change shape and character. Maybe it can project itself to a distance—which makes it all the harder, both for us to face it and for us to get help."

"I know what you mean by that last," I nodded gloomily. "If there were ten thousand friendly constables in the neighborhood, instead of a single hostile one, they wouldn't believe us."

"Right," agreed Judge Pursuivant. "We're like the group of perplexed mortals in *Dracula*, who had only their own wits and weapons against a monster no more forbidding than ours."

* * * *

It is hard to show clearly how his constant offering of parallels and rationalizations comforted us. Only the unknown and unknowable can terrify completely. We three were even cheerful over a bottle of wine that William fetched and poured out in three glasses. Judge Pursuivant gave us a toast—"May wolves go hungry!"—and Susan and I drank it gladly.

"Don't forget what's on our side," said the judge, putting down his glass. "I mean the stedfast and courageous heart, of which I preached to Wills last night, and which we can summon from within us any time and anywhere. The werewolf, dauntlessly faced, loses its dread; and I think we are the ones to face it. Now we're ready for action."

I said that I would welcome any kind of action whatsoever, and Susan touched my arm as if in endorsement of the remark, Judge Pursuivant's spectacles glittered in approval.

"You two will go into the Devil's Croft," he announced. "I'm going back to town once more."

"Into the Devil's Croft!" we almost shouted, both in the same shocked breath.

"Of course. Didn't we just get through with the agreement all around that the lycanthrope can and must be met face to face? Offense is the best defense, as perhaps one hundred thousand athletic trainers have reiterated."

"I've already faced the creature once," I reminded him. "As for appearing dauntless, I doubt my own powers of deceit."

"You shall have a weapon," he said. "A fire gives light, and we know that such things must have darkness—such as it finds in the midst of that swampy wood. So fill your pockets with matches, both of you."

"How about a gun?" I asked, but he shook his head.

"We don't want the werewolf killed. That would leave the whole business in mystery, and yourself probably charged with another murder. He'd return to his human shape, you know, the moment he was hurt even slightly."

Susan spoke, very calmly: "I'm ready to go into the Croft, Judge Pursuivant."

He clapped his hands loudly, as if applauding in a theater. "Bravo, my dear, bravo! I see Mr. Wills sets his jaw. That means he's ready to go with you. Very well, let us be off."

He called to William, who at his orders brought three lanterns—sturdy old-fashioned affairs, protected by strong wire nettings—and filled them with oil. We each took one and set out. It had turned clear and frosty once more, and the moon shone too brightly for my comfort, at least. However, as we approached the grove, we saw no sentinels; they could hardly be blamed for deserting, after the fate of the younger O'Bryant.

We gained the shadow of the outer cedars unchallenged. Here Judge Pursuivant called a halt, produced a match from his overcoat pocket and lighted our lanterns all around. I remember that we struck a fresh light for Susan's lantern; we agreed that, silly as the three-on-a-match superstition might be, this was no time or place to tempt Providence.

"Come on," said Judge Pursuivant then, and led the way into the darkest part of the immense thicket.

CHAPTER 12

"WE ARE HERE AT HIS MERCY."

We followed Judge Pursuivant, Susan and I, without much of a thought beyond an understandable dislike for being left alone on the brink of the timber. It was a slight struggle to get through the close-set cedar hedge, especially for Susan, but beyond it we soon caught up with the judge. He strode heavily and confidently among the trees, his lantern held high to shed light upon broad, polished leaves and thick, wet stems. The moist warmth of the grove's interior made itself felt again, and the judge explained again and at greater length the hot springs that made possible this surprizing condition. All the while he kept going. He seemed to know his way in that forbidden fastness—indeed, he must have explored it many times to go straight to his destination.

That destination was a clearing, in some degree like the one where I had met and fought with my hairy pursuer on the night before. This place had, however, a great tree in its center, with branches that shot out in all directions to hide away the sky completely. By straining the ears one could catch a faint murmur of water—my scalding stream, no doubt. Around us were the thick-set trunks of the forest, filled in between with brush and vines, and underfoot grew velvety moss.

"This will be our headquarters position," said the judge. "Wills, help me gather wood for a fire. Break dead branches from the standing trees—never mind picking up wood from the ground, it will be too damp."

Together we collected a considerable heap and, crumpling a bit of paper in its midst, he kindled it.

"Now, then," he went on, "I'm heading for town. You two will stay here and keep each other company."

He took our lanterns, blew them out and ran his left arm through the loops of their handles.

"I'm sure that nothing will attack you in the light of the fire. You're bound to attract whatever skulks hereabouts, however. When I come back, we ought to be prepared to go into the final act of our little melodrama."

He touched my hand, bowed to Susan, and went tramping away into the timber. The thick leafage blotted his lantern-light from our view before his back had been turned twenty seconds.

Susan and I gazed at each other, and smiled rather uneasily.

"It's warm," she breathed, and took off her cloak. Dropping it upon one of the humped roots of the great central tree, she sat down on it with her back to the trunk. "What kind of a tree is this?"

I gazed up at the gnarled stem, or as much of it as I could see in the firelight. Finally I shook my head.

"I don't know—I'm no expert," I admitted. "At least it's very big, and undoubtedly very old—the sort of tree that used to mark a place of sacrifice."

At the word "sacrifice," Susan lifted her shoulders as if in distaste. "You're right, Talbot. It would be something grim and Druid-like." She began to recite, half to herself:

> That tree in whose dark shadow
> The ghastly priest doth reign,
> The priest who slew the slayer
> And shall himself be slain.

"Macaulay," I said at once. Then, to get her mind off of morbid things, "I had to recite *The Lays of Ancient Rome* in school, when I was a boy. I wish you hadn't mentioned it."

"You mean, because it's an evil omen?" She shook her head, and contrived a smile that lighted up her pale face. "It's not that, if you analyze it. 'Shall himself be slain'—it sounds as if the enemy's fate is sealed."

I nodded, then spun around sharply, for I fancied I heard a dull crashing at the edge of the clearing. Then I went here and there, gathering wood enough to keep our fire burning for some time. One branch, a thick, straight one, I chose from the heap and leaned against the big tree, within easy reach of my hand.

"That's for a club," I told Susan, and she half shrunk, half stiffened at the implication.

We fell to talking about Judge Pursuivant, the charm and the enigma that invested him. Both of us felt gratitude that he had immediately clarified our own innocence in the grisly slayings, but to both came a sudden inspiration, distasteful and disquieting. I spoke first:

"Susan! Why did the judge bring us here?"

"He said, to help face and defeat the monster. But—but—"

"Who is that monster?" I demanded. "What human being puts on a semi-bestial appearance, to rend and kill?"

"Y—you don't mean the judge?"

As I say, it had been in both our minds. We were silent, and felt shame and embarrassment.

"Look here," I went on earnestly after a moment, "perhaps we're being ungrateful, but we mustn't be unprepared. Think, Susan; nobody knows where Judge Pursuivant was at the time of your father's death, at the time I saw the thing in these woods." I broke off, remembering how I had met the judge for the first time, so shortly after my desperate struggle with the point-eared demon. "Nobody knows where he was when the constable's brother was attacked and mortally wounded."

She gazed about fearfully. "Nobody," she added breathlessly, "knows where he is now."

I was remembering a conversation with him; he had spoken of books, mentioning a rare, a supposedly non-existent volume. What was it?...the *Wicked Bible*. And what was it I had once heard about that work?

It came back to me now, out of the sub-conscious brain-chamber where, apparently, one stores everything he hears or reads in idleness, and from which such items creep on occasion. It had been in Lewis Spence's *Encyclopedia of Occultism*, now on the shelf in my New York apartment.

The *Wicked Bible*, scripture for witches and wizards, from which magic-mongers of the Dark Ages drew their inspiration and their knowledge! And Judge Pursuivant had admitted to having one!

What had he learned from it? How had he been so glib about the science—yes, and the psychology—of being a werewolf?

"If what we suspect is true," I said to Susan, "we are here at his mercy. Nobody is going to come in here, not if horses dragged them. At his leisure he will fall upon us and tear us to pieces."

But, even as I spoke, I despised myself for my weak fears in her presence. I picked up my club and was comforted by its weight and thickness.

"I met that devil once," I said, studying cheer and confidence into my voice this time. "I don't think it relished the meeting any too much. Next time won't be any more profitable for it."

She smiled at me, as if in comradely encouragement; then we both started and fell silent. There had risen, somewhere among the thickets, a long low whining.

* * * *

I put out a foot, stealthily, as though fearful of being caught in motion. A quick kick flung more wood on the fire. I blinked in the light and felt the heat. Standing there, as a primitive man might have stood in his flame-guarded camp to face the horrors of the ancient world, I tried to judge by ear the direction of that whine.

It died, and I heard, perhaps in my imagination, a stealthy padding. Then the whining began again, from a new quarter and nearer.

I made myself step toward it. My shadow, leaping grotesquely among the tree trunks, almost frightened me out of my wits. The whine had changed into a crooning wail, such as that with which dogs salute the full moon. It seemed to plead, to promise; and it was coming closer to the clearing.

Once before I had challenged and taunted the thing with scornful words. Now I could not make my lips form a single syllable. Probably it was just as well, for I thought and watched the more. Something black and cautious was moving among the branches, just beyond the shrubbery that screened it from our firelight. I knew, without need of a clear view, what that black something was. I lifted my club to the ready.

The sound it made had become in some fashion articulate, though not human in any quality. There were no words to it, but it spoke to the heart. The note of plea and promise had become one of command—and not directed to me.

I found my own voice.

"Get out of here, you devil!" I roared at it, and threw my club. Even as I let go of it, I wished I had not. The bushes foiled my aim, and the missile crashed among them and dropped to the mossy ground. The creature fell craftily silent. Then I felt sudden panic and regret at being left weaponless, and I retreated toward the fire.

"Susan," I said huskily, "give me another stick. Hurry!"

She did not move or stir, and I rummaged frantically among the heaped dry branches for myself. Catching up the first piece of wood that would serve, I turned to her with worried curiosity.

She was still seated upon the cloak-draped root, but she had drawn herself tense, like a cat before a mouse-hole. Her head was thrust forward, so far that her neck extended almost horizontally. Her dilated eyes were turned in the direction from which the whining and crooning had come. They had a strange clarity in them, as if they could pierce the twigs and leaves and meet there an answering, understanding gaze.

"Susan!" I cried.

Still she gave no sign that she heard me, if hear me she did. She leaned farther forward, as if ready to spring up and run. Once more the unbeastly wail rose from the place where our watcher was lurking.

Susan's lips trembled. From them came slowly and softly, then louder, a long-drawn answering howl.

"*Aoooooooooooooo! Aooooooooooooooooooooo!*"

The stick almost fell from my hands. She rose, slowly but confidently. Her shoulders hunched high, her arms hung forward as though they wanted to reach to the ground. Again she howled:

"*Aoooooooooooooooooooooo!*"

I saw that she was going to move across the clearing, toward the trees—through the trees. My heart seemed to twist into a knot inside me, but I could not let her do such a thing. I made a quick stride and planted myself before her.

"Susan, you mustn't!"

She shrank back, her face turning slowly up to mine. Her back was to the fire, yet light rose in her eyes, or perhaps behind them; a green light, such as reflects in still forest pools from the moon. Her hands lifted suddenly, as though to repel me. They were half closed and the crooked fingers drawn stiff, like talons.

"Susan!" I coaxed her, yet again, and she made no answer but tried to slip sidewise around me. I moved and headed her off, and she growled—actually growled, like a savage dog.

With my free hand I clutched her shoulder. Under my fingers her flesh was as taut as wire fabric. Then, suddenly, it relaxed into human tissue again, and she was standing straight. Her eyes had lost their weird light, they showed only dark and frightened.

"Talbot," she stammered. "Wh—what have I been doing?"

"Nothing, my dear," I comforted her. "It was nothing that we weren't able to fight back."

From the woods behind me came a throttling yelp, as of some hungry thing robbed of prey within its very grasp. Susan swayed, seemed about to drop, and I caught her quickly in my arms. Holding her thus, I turned my head and laughed over my shoulder.

"Another score against you!" I jeered at my enemy. "You didn't get her, not with all your filthy enchantments!"

Susan was beginning to cry, and I half led, half carried her back to the fireside. At my gesture she sat on her cloak again, as tractable as a child who repents of rebellion and tries to be obedient.

There were no more sounds from the timber. I could feel an emptiness there, as if the monster had slunk away, baffled.

CHAPTER 13

"LIGHT'S OUR BEST WEAPON."

Neither of us said anything for a while after that. I stoked up the fire, to be doing something, and it made us so uncomfortably warm that we had to crowd away from it. Sitting close against the tree-trunk, I began to imagine something creeping up the black lane of shadow it cast behind us to the edge of the clearing; and yet again I thought I heard noises. Club in hand, I went to investigate, and I was not disappointed in the least when I found nothing.

Finally Susan spoke. "This," she said, "is a new light on the thing."

"It's nothing to be upset about," I tried to comfort her.

"Not be upset!" She sat straight up, and in the light of the fire I could see a single pained line between her brows, deep and sharp as a chisel-gash. "Not when I almost turned into a beast!"

"How much of that do you remember?" I asked her.

"I was foggy in my mind, Talbot, almost as at the séance, but I remember being drawn—drawn to what was waiting out there." Her eyes sought the thickets on the far side of our blaze. "And it didn't seem horrible, but pleasant and welcome and—well, as if it were my kind. You," and she glanced quickly at me, then ashamedly away, "you were suddenly strange and to be avoided."

"Is that all?"

"It spoke to me," she went on in husky horror, "and I spoke to it."

I forbore to remind her that the only sound she had uttered was a wordless howl. Perhaps she did not know that—I hoped not. We said no more for another awkward time.

Finally she mumbled, "I'm not the kind of woman who cries easily; but I'd like to now."

"Go ahead," I said at once, and she did, and I let her. Whether I took her into my arms, or whether she came into them of her own accord, I do not remember exactly; but it was against my shoulder that she finished her weeping, and when she had finished she did feel better.

"That somehow washed the fog and the fear out of me," she confessed, almost brightly.

It must have been a full hour later that rustlings rose yet again in the timber. So frequently had my imagination tricked me that I did not so much as glance up. Then Susan gave a little startled cry, and I sprang to my feet. Beyond the fire a tall, gray shape had become visible, with a pale glare of light around it.

"Don't be alarmed," called a voice I knew. "It is I—Otto Zoberg."

"Doctor!" I cried, and hurried to meet him. For the first time in my life, I felt that he was a friend. Our differences of opinion, once making companionship strained, had so dwindled to nothing in comparison to the danger I faced, and his avowed trust in me as innocent of murder.

"How are you?" I said, wringing his hand. "They say you were hurt by the mob."

"*Ach*, it was nothing serious," he reassured me. "Only this." He touched with his forefinger an eye, and I could see that it was bruised and swollen half shut. "A citizen with too ready a fist and too slow a mind has that to answer for."

"I'm partly responsible," I said. "You were trying to help me, I understand, when it happened."

* * * *

More noise behind him, and two more shapes pushed into the clearing. I recognized Judge Pursuivant, nodding to me with his eyes bright under his wide hat-brim. The other man, angular, falcon-faced, one arm in a sling, I had also seen before. It was Constable O'Bryant. I spoke to him, but he gazed past me, apparently not hearing.

Doctor Zoberg saw my perplexed frown, and he turned back toward the constable. Snapping long fingers in front of the great hooked nose, he whistled shrilly. O'Bryant started, grunted, then glared around as though he had been suddenly and rudely awakened.

"What's up?" he growled menacingly, and his sound hand moved swiftly to a holster at his side. Then his eyes found me, and with an oath he drew his revolver.

"Easy, Constable! Easy does it," soothed Judge Pursuivant, his own great hand clutching O'Bryant's wrist. "You've forgotten that I showed how Mr. Wills must be innocent."

"I've forgotten what we're here for at all," snapped O'Bryant, gazing around the clearing. "Hey, have I been drunk or something? I said that I'd never—"

"I'll explain," offered Zoberg. "The judge met me in town, and we came together to see you. Remember? You said you would like to avenge your brother's death, and came with us. Then, when you balked at the very edge of this Devil's Croft, I took the liberty of hypnotizing you."

"Huh? How did you do that?" growled the officer.

"With a look, a word, a motion of the hand," said Zoberg, his eyes twinkling. "Then you ceased all objections and came in with us."

Pursuivant clapped O'Bryant on the unwounded shoulder. "Sit down," he invited, motioning toward the roots of the tree.

The five of us gathered around the fire, like picknickers instead of allies against a supernormal monster. There, at Susan's insistence, I told of what had happened since Judge Pursuivant had left us. All listened with rapt attention, the constable grunting occasionally, the judge clicking his tongue, and Doctor Zoberg in absolute silence.

It was Zoberg who made the first comment after I had finished. "This explains many things," he said.

"It don't explain a doggone thing," grumbled O'Bryant.

Zoberg smiled at him, then turned to Judge Pursuivant. "Your ectoplasmic theory of lycanthropy—such as you have explained it to me—is most interesting and, I think, valid. May I advance it a trifle?"

"In what way?" asked the judge.

"Ectoplasm, as you see it, forms the werewolf by building upon the medium's body. But is not ectoplasm more apt, according to the observations of many people, to draw completely away and form a separate and complete thing of itself? The thing may be beastly, as you suggest. Algernon Blackwood, the English writer of psychic stories, almost hits upon it in one of his 'John Silence' tales. He described an astral personality taking form and threatening harm while its physical body slept."

"I know the story you mean," agreed Judge Pursuivant. "*The Camp of the Dog*, I think it's called."

"Very well, then. Perhaps, while Miss Susan's body lay in a trance, securely handcuffed between Wills and myself—"

"Oh!" wailed Susan. "Then it was I, after all."

"It couldn't have been you," I told her at once.

"But it was! And, while I was at the judge's home with you, part of me met the constable's brother in this wood." She stared wildly around her.

"It might as well have been part of *me*," I argued, and O'Bryant glared at me as if in sudden support of that likelihood. But Susan shook her head.

"No, for which of us responded to the call of that thing out there?"

For the hundredth time she gazed fearfully through the fire at the bushes behind which the commanding whine had risen.

"I have within me," she said dully, "a nature that will break out, look and act like a beast-demon, will kill even my beloved father—"

"Please," interjected Judge Pursuivant earnestly, "you must not take responsibility upon yourself for what happened. If the ectoplasm engendered by you made up the form of the killer, the spirit may have come from without."

"How could it?" she asked wretchedly.

"How could Marthe Beraud exude ectoplasm that formed a bearded, masculine body?" Pursuivant looked across to Zoberg. "Doctor, you surely know the famous 'Bien Boa' séance, and how the materialized entity spoke Arabic when the medium, a Frenchwoman, knew little or nothing of that language?"

Zoberg sat with bearded chin on lean hand. His joined brows bristled the more as he corrugated his forehead in thought. "We are each a thousand personalities," he said, sententiously if not comfortingly. "How can we rule them all, or rule even one of them?"

* * * *

O'Bryant said sourly that all this talk was too high flown for him to understand or to enjoy. He dared hope, however, that the case could never be tied up to Miss Susan Gird, whom he had known and liked since her babyhood.

"It can never do that," Zoberg said definitely. "No court or jury would convict her on the evidence we are offering against her."

I ventured an opinion: "While you are attempting to show that Susan is a werewolf, you are forgetting that something else was prowling around our fire, just out of sight."

"*Ach*, just out of sight!" echoed Zoberg. "That means you aren't sure what it was."

"Or even that there was anything," added Susan, so suddenly and strongly that I, at least, jumped.

"There was something, all right," I insisted. "I heard it."

"You thought you heard a sound behind the tree," Susan reminded me. "You looked, and there was nothing."

Everyone gazed at me, rather like staid adults at a naughty child. I said, ungraciously, that my imagination was no better than theirs, and that I was no easier to frighten. Judge Pursuivant suggested that we make a search of the surrounding woods, for possible clues.

"A good idea," approved Constable O'Bryant. "The ground's damp. We might find some sort of footprints."

"Then you stay here with Miss Susan," the judge said to him. "We others will circle around."

The gaunt constable shook his head. "Not much, mister. I'm in on whatever searching is done. I've got something to settle with whatever killed my kid brother."

"But there are only three lanterns," pointed out Judge Pursuivant. "We have to carry them—light's our best weapon."

Zoberg then spoke up, rather diffidently, to say that he would be glad to stay with Susan. This was agreed upon, and the other three of us prepared for the search.

I took the lantern from Zoberg's hand, nodded to the others, and walked away among the trees.

CHAPTER 14

"I WAS—I AM—A WOLF."

Deliberately I had turned my face toward the section beyond the fire, for, as I have said repeatedly, it was there that I had heard the movements and cries of the being that had so strongly moved and bewitched Susan. My heart whispered rather loudly that I must look for myself at its traces or lack of them, or for ever view myself with scorn.

Almost at once I found tracks, the booted tracks of my three allies. Shaking my lantern to make it flare higher, I went deeper among the clumps, my eyes quartering the damp earth. After a few moments I found what I had come to look for.

The marks were round and rather vague as to toe-positions, yet not so clear-cut as to be made by hoofs. Rather they suggested a malformed stump or a palm with no fingers, and they were deep enough to denote considerable weight; the tracks of my own shoes, next to them, were rather shallower. I bent for a close look, then straightened up, looked everywhere at once, and held my torch above my head to shed light all around; for I had suddenly felt eyes upon me.

I caught just a glimpse as of two points of light, fading away into some leafage and in the direction of the clearing, and toward them I made my way; but there was nothing there, and the only tracks underfoot were of shod human beings, myself or one of the others. I returned to my outward search, following the round tracks.

They were plainly of only two feet—there were no double impressions, like those of a quadruped—but I must have stalked along them for ten minutes when I realized that I had no way of telling whether they went forward or backward. I might be going away from my enemy instead of toward it. A close examination did me little good, and I further pondered that the creature would lurk near the clearing, not go so straight away. Thus arguing within myself, I doubled back.

Coming again close to the starting-point, I thought of a quick visit to the clearing and a comforting word or two with Susan and Zoberg. Surely I was almost there; but why did not the fire gleam through the trees? Were they out of wood? Perplexed, I quickened my pace. A gnarled tree grew in my path, its low branches heavily bearded with vines. Beyond this rose only the faintest of glows. I paused to push aside some strands and peer.

The fire had almost died, and by its light I but half saw two figures, one tall and one slender, standing together well to one side. They faced each other, and the taller—a seeming statue of wet-looking gray—held its companion by a shoulder. The other gray hand was stroking the smaller one's head, pouring grayness thereon.

I saw only this much, without stopping to judge or to wonder. Then I yelled, and sprang into the clearing. At my outcry the two fell apart and faced me. The smallest was Susan, who took a step in my direction and gave a little smothered whimper, as though she was trying to speak through a blanket. I ran to her side, and with a rough sweep of my sleeve I cleared from her face and head a mass of slimy, shiny jelly.

"You!" I challenged the other shape. "What have you been trying to do to her?"

For only a breathing-space it stood still, as featureless and clumsy as a half-formed figure of gray mud. Then darkness sprang out upon it, and hair. Eyes blazed at me, green and fearsome. A sharp muzzle opened to emit a snarl.

"Now I know you," I hurled at it. "I'm going to kill you."

And I charged.

Claws ripped at my head, missed and tore the cloth of my coat. One of my arms shot around a lean, hairy middle with powerful muscles straining under its skin, and I drove my other fist for where I judged the pit of the stomach to be. Grappled, we fell and rolled over. The beast smell I remembered was all about us, and I knew that jaws were shoving once again at my throat. I jammed my forearm between them, so far into the hinge of them that they could not close nor crush. My other hand clutched the skin of the throat, a great loose fistful, drew it taut and began to twist with all my strength. I heard a half-broken yelp of strangled pain, felt a slackening of the body that struggled against me, knew that it was trying to get away. But I managed to roll on top, straddling the thing.

"You're not so good on defense," I panted, and brought my other hand to the throat, for I had no other idea save to kill. Paws grasped and tore at my wrists. There was shouting at my back, in Susan's voice and several others. Hands caught me by the shoulders and tried to pull me up and away.

"No!" I cried. "This is it, the werewolf!"

"It's Doctor Zoberg, you idiot," growled O'Bryant in my ear. "Come on, let him up."

"Yes," added Judge Pursuivant, "it's Doctor Zoberg, as you say; but a moment ago it was the monster we have been hunting."

I had been dragged upright by now, and so had Zoberg. He could only choke and glare for the time being, his fingers to his half-crushed throat. Pursuivant had moved within clutching distance of him, and was eyeing him as a cat eyes a mouse.

"Like Wills, I only pretended to search, then doubled back to watch," went on the judge. "I saw Zoberg and Miss Susan talking. He spoke quietly, rhythmically, commandingly. She went into half a trance, and I knew she was hypnotized.

"As the fire died down, he began the change. Ectoplasm gushed out and over him. Before it took form, he began to smear some upon her. And Mr. Wills here came out of the woods and at him."

O'Bryant looked from the judge to Zoberg. Then he fumbled with his undamaged hand in a hip pocket, produced handcuffs and stepped forward. The accused man grinned through his beard, as if admitting defeat in some trifling game. Then he held out his wrists with an air of resignation and I, who had manacled them once, wondered again at their corded strength. The irons clicked shut upon one, then the other.

"You know everything now," said Zoberg, in a soft voice but a steady one. "I was—I am—a wolf; a wolf who hoped to mate with an angel."

His bright eyes rested upon Susan, who shrank back. Judge Pursuivant took a step toward the prisoner.

"There is no need for you to insult her," he said.

Zoberg grinned at him, with every long tooth agleam. "Do you want to hear my confession, or don't you?"

"Sure we want to hear it," grunted O'Bryant. "Leave him alone, judge, and let him talk." He glanced at me. "Got any paper, Mr. Wills? Somebody better take this down in writing."

I produced a wad of note-paper and a stub pencil. Placing it upon my knee, with the lantern for light, I scribbled, almost word for word, the tale that Doctor Zoberg told.

CHAPTER 15

"AND THAT IS THE END."

"Perhaps I was born what I am," he began. "At least, even as a lad I knew that there was a lust and a power for evil within me. Night called to me, where it frightens most children. I would slip out of my father's house and run for miles, under the trees or across fields, with the moon for company. This was in Germany, of course, before the war."

"During the war—" began Judge Pursuivant.

"During the war, when most men were fighting, I was in prison." Again Zoberg grinned, briefly and without cheer. "I had found it easy and inspiring to kill persons, with a sense of added strength following. But they caught me and put me in what they called an asylum. I was supposed to be crazy. They confined me closely, but I, reading books in the library, grew to know what the change was that came upon me at certain intervals. I turned my attention to it, and became able to control the change, bringing it on or holding it off at will."

He looked at Susan again. "But I'm ahead of my story. Once, when I was at school, I met a girl—an American student of science and philosophy. She laughed at my wooing, but talked to me about spirits and psychical phenomena. That, my dear Susan, was your mother. When the end of the war brought so many new things, it also brought a different viewpoint toward many inmates of asylums. Some Viennese doctors, and later Sigmund Freud himself, found my case interesting. Of course, they did not arrive at the real truth, or they would not have procured my release."

"After that," I supplied, writing swiftly, "you became an expert psychical investigator and journeyed to America."

"Yes, to find the girl who had once laughed and studied with me. After some years I came to this town, simply to trace the legend of this Devil's Croft. And here, I found, she had lived and died, and left behind a daughter that was her image."

Judge Pursuivant cleared his throat. "I suspect that you're leaving out part of your adventures, Doctor."

Zoberg actually laughed. "*Ja*, I thought to spare you a few shocks. But if you will have them, you may. I visited Russia—and in 1922 a medical commission of the Soviet Union investigated several score mysterious cases of peasants killed—and eaten." He licked his lips, like a cat who thinks of meat. "In Paris I founded and conducted a rather interesting night school, for the study of diabolism in its relationship to science. And in 1936, certain summer vacationists on Long Island were almost frightened out of their wits by a lurking thing that seemed half beast, half man." He chuckled. "Your *Literary Digest* made much of it. The lurking thing was, of course, myself."

We stared. "Say, why do you do these things?" the constable blurted.

Zoberg turned to him, head quizzically aslant. "Why do you uphold your local laws? Or why does Judge Pursuivant study ancient philosophies? Or why do Wills and Susan turn soft eyes upon each other? Because the heart of each so insists."

Susan was clutching my arm. Her fingers bit into my flesh as Zoberg's eyes sought her again.

"I found the daughter of someone I once loved," he went on, with real gentleness in his voice. "Wills, at least, can see in her what I saw. A new inspiration came to me, a wish and a plan to have a comrade in my secret exploits."

"A beast-thing like yourself?" prompted the judge.

Zoberg nodded. "A *lupa* to my *lupus*. But this girl—Susan Gird—had not inherited the psychic possibilities of her mother."

"What!" I shouted. "You yourself said that she was the greatest medium of all time!"

"I did say so. But it was a lie."

"Why, in heaven's name—"

"It was my hope," he broke in quietly, "to make of her a medium, or a lycanthrope—call the phenomenon which you will. Are you interested in my proposed method?" He gazed mockingly around, and his eyes rested finally upon me. "Make full notes, Wills. This will be interesting, if not stupefying, to the psychic research committees.

"It is, as you know, a supernormal substance that is exuded to change the appearance of my body. What, I wondered, would some of that substance do if smeared upon her?"

I started to growl out a curse upon him, but Judge Pursuivant, rapt, motioned for me to keep silent.

"Think back through all the demonologies you have read," Zoberg was urging. "What of the strange 'witch ointments' that, spread over an ordinary human body, gave it beast-form and beast-heart? There, again, legend had basis in scientific fact."

"By the thunder, you're logical," muttered Judge Pursuivant.

"And damnable," I added. "Go on, Doctor. You were going to smear the change-stuff upon Susan."

"But first, I knew, I must convince her that she had within her the essence of a wolf. And so, the séances."

"She was no medium," I said again.

"I made her think she was. I hypnotized her, and myself did weird wonders in the dark room. But she, in a trance, did not know. I needed witnesses to convince her."

"So you invited Mr. Wills," supplied Judge Pursuivant.

"Yes, and her father. They had been prepared to accept her as medium and me as observer. Seeing a beast-form, they would tell her afterward that it was she."

"Zoberg," I said between set teeth, "you're convicted out of your own mouth of rottenness that convinces me of the existence of the Devil after whom this grove was named. I wish to heaven that I'd killed you when we were fighting."

"*Ach*, Wills," he chuckled, "you'd have missed this most entertaining autobiographical lecture."

"He's right," grumbled O'Bryant; and, "Let him go on," the judge pleaded with me.

* * * *

"Once sure of this power within her," Zoberg said deeply, "she would be prepared in heart and soul to change at touch of the ointment—the ectoplasm. Then, to me she must turn as a fellow-creature. Together, throughout the world, adventuring in a way unbelievable—"

His voice died, and we let it. He stood in the firelight, head thrown back, manacled hands folded. He might have been a martyr instead of a fiend for whom a death at the stake would be too easy.

"I can tell what spoiled the séance," I told him after a moment. "Gird, sitting opposite, saw that it was you, not Susan, who had changed. You had to kill him to keep him from telling, there and then."

"Yes," agreed Zoberg. "After that, you were arrested, and, later, threatened. I was in an awkward position. Susan must believe herself, not you, guilty. That is why I have championed you throughout. I went then to look for you."

"And attacked me," I added.

"The beast-self was ascendant. I cannot always control it completely." He sighed. "When Susan disappeared, I went to look for her on the second evening. When I came into this wood, the change took place, half automatically. Associations, I suppose. Constable, your brother happened upon me in an evil hour."

"Yep," said O'Bryant gruffly.

"And that is the end," Zoberg said. "The end of the story and, I suppose, the end of me."

"You bet it is," the constable assured him. "You came with the judge to finish your rotten work. But we're finishing it for you."

"One moment," interjected Judge Pursuivant, and his fire-lit face betrayed a perplexed frown. "The story fails to explain one important thing."

"Does it so?" prompted Zoberg, inclining toward him with a show of negligent grace.

"If you were able to free yourself and kill Mr. Gird—"

"By heaven, that's right!" I broke in. "You were chained, Zoberg, to Susan and to your chair. I'd go bail for the strength and tightness of those handcuffs."

He grinned at each of us in turn and held out his hands with their manacles. "Is it not obvious?" he inquired.

We looked at him, a trifle blankly I suppose, for he chuckled once again.

"Another employment of the ectoplasm, that useful substance of change," he said gently. "At will my arms and legs assume thickness, and hold the rings of the confining irons wide. Then, when I wish, they grow slender again, and—"

He gave his hands a sudden flirt, and the bracelets fell from them on the instant. He pivoted and ran like a deer.

"Shoot!" cried the judge, and O'Bryant whipped the big gun from his holster.

Zoberg was almost within a vine-laced clump of bushes when O'Bryant fired. I heard a shrill scream, and saw Zoberg falter and drop to his hands and knees.

We were all starting forward. I paused a moment to put Susan behind me, and in that moment O'Bryant and Pursuivant sprang ahead and came up on either side of Zoberg. He was still alive, for he writhed up to a kneeling position and made a frantic clutch at the judge's coat. O'Bryant, so close that he barely raised his hand and arm, fired a second time.

Zoberg spun around somehow on his knees, stiffened and screamed. Perhaps I should say that he howled. In his voice was the inarticulate agony of a beast wounded to death. Then he collapsed.

Both men stooped above him, cautious but thorough in their examination. Finally Judge Pursuivant straightened up and faced toward us.

"Keep Miss Susan there with you," he warned me. "He's dead, and not a pretty sight."

Slowly they came back to us. Pursuivant was thoughtful, while O'Bryant, Zoberg's killer, seemed cheerful for the first time since I had met him. He even smiled at me, as Punch would smile after striking a particularly telling blow with his cudgel. Rubbing his pistol caressingly with his palm, he stowed it carefully away.

"I'm glad that's over," he admitted. "My brother can rest easy in his grave."

"And we have our work cut out for us," responded the judge. "We must decide just how much of the truth to tell when we make a report."

O'Bryant dipped his head in sage acquiescence. "You're right," he rumbled. "Yes, sir, you're right."

"Would you believe me," said the judge, "if I told you that I knew it was Zoberg, almost from the first?"

But Susan and I, facing each other, were beyond being surprised, even at that.